MERLIN FIGHTS A GHOST

MOLLY FITZ

© 2021, Molly Fitz.

All rights reserved. Except as permitted under the U.S. Copyright Act of 1976, no part of this publication may be reproduced, distributed or transmitted in any form or by any means, or stored in a database or retrieval system without the prior written permission of the publisher.

Editor: Jennifer Lopez, Mistress with the Red Pen

Cover & Graphics Designer: Amala Benny, Mayflower Studio

This is a work of fiction. Names, characters, organizations, places, events, and incidents are either products of the author's imagination or are used fictitiously. Any resemblance to actual persons, living or dead, or actual events is purely coincidental.

No part of this work may be reproduced, or stored in a retrieval system, or transmitted in any form or by any means, electronic, mechanical, photocopying, recording, or otherwise, without written permission of the publisher.

Whiskered Mysteries
PO Box 72
Brighton, MI 48116

AUTHOR'S NOTE

Hey, new reader friend!

Welcome to the crazy inner workings of my brain. I hope you'll find it a fun and exciting place to be.

If you love snarky talking animals and crazy magical mishaps as much as I do, then I'm pretty sure you're going to enjoy the journey ahead.

This book is just one of my many brain-tickling adventures to come, so make sure you keep in touch to keep in the know!

I've done my best to make it easy by offering several fun ways to access sneak peeks of upcoming books, monthly giveaways, adorable pictures of my own personal feline overlords, and many other cool things that are just for my inner circle of readers.

So take a quick moment now to choose your favorite:

Download my app
Join my VIP reader group
Sign up for my newsletter
Kick off a cat chat on Facebook

Okay, ready to talk to some animals and solve some mysteries?

Let's do this!
    Molly Fitz

1

Hello, I'm Gracie Springs. I used to be a pretty normal girl, until about a week ago. You see, my boss got murdered by magic, then an evil witch and her accomplice tried to frame me for it.

As it turns out, I'm descended from King Arthur. I've also been chosen to serve as my witchy cat's familiar. I used to call him Fluffy, but now I know he much prefers to go by Merlin. He has a famous lineage, too. He's descended from the original Merlin.

No, not the human imposter everyone thinks they know. The real wizard, who just so happened to be a cat.

Because of our intertwined ancestry, Merlin

and I have an almost unbreakable bond. Almost.

The bad guy got away last time, but we both know she'll be back with a new plan to steal Merlin's magic from him for good.

While all this has been going on, I've also needed to keep up the appearances of a normal life by working my part-time barista job at Harold's House of Coffee. The shop is in the process of being remodeled, thanks to the very ambitious goals of Harold's successor, his long-lost daughter, Kelley.

Also, I'm very close to completing my master's degree in Sociology. I just have to finish my thesis, and then I can find work in my field rather than forever working as a part-time bean-slinger.

Lately, though, I'm plenty busy with getting the hang of my new role as a familiar. Both Merlin and his new girlfriend are more than happy to grill me at all hours of the day and night.

I need to be ready for when the next magical attack happens, and make no mistake, we all know it's coming soon.

I bet my grandma never would have

guessed what was in store for me when she gifted me her small-town Georgia home and retired to the Florida Keys. She certainly didn't know that a certain magical Maine Coon had already been scoping her out to work as his familiar, or that he'd later choose me in her place.

Honestly, even though my life has taken a turn for the crazy, I wouldn't have it any other way. I love Merlin, and I love our adventures together, no matter how much they frighten the frijoles out of me.

I can't cast magic, but that doesn't mean I'm not important in our fight against the wicked illusion witch who has set her sights on us.

But this time when she finds us, I'll be ready to take her down.

An unholy shriek woke me from a dead sleep.

Meeeeeeeeeeeh!

I darted upright in bed and grabbed my cell phone to serve as a flashlight. "Who's there?" I demanded.

But was only answered by Merlin

thumping down the hardwood floor in the hallway.

Meeeeeeeeeh! the shriek sounded again, and this time I realized it was Luna crying her heart out.

And so it went. Shriek, scamper. Shriek, scamper. Until at last I made my way into the hall and found them both staring at the far corner of the ceiling with their ears pressed back against their little kitty heads.

"What's going on?" I asked, knowing full well both of them were capable of more than just uncivilized meows.

"Gh-gh-gh-ghost," Merlin said, then took another sprint down the short hallway.

I glanced up to the spot where Luna still had her large unblinking eyes fixed... and saw absolutely nothing.

Still, I asked her, "What do you see?" Generally, she was the more logical of the two—or at least the one more likely to open up to me.

"I can't see anything," she whispered without removing her gaze from the ceiling. "But there's an energy that's forming. It's not wholly in our world yet. It will be soon, though."

"So you see a pre-ghost?" I summarized.

"Something like that."

"But how can you tell? You're not magical anymore," I reminded her.

Luna couldn't stifle the hiss that escaped her. "I may not be a witch, but I am still a cat. Magical or not, we can all see into the supernatural realm."

"Like Nocturna?" I asked, referring to the magical nighttime city that was only accessible to magical creatures at the twilight hour.

Merlin growled and began to kick up his hind legs.

"Oh, no, you don't!" I cried, reaching down to pluck him into my arms. "No tornadoes inside the house."

He growled in dismay until I set him back down.

"We must get rid of it before it takes its full form," Luna told me as she worried her bottom lip with her top fangs.

"The fact that it's here so soon in its after-life journey is a very bad sign," Merlin revealed, and when I looked down at him he had arched his back and puffed up to maximum volume.

I grabbed him into my arms again. "Definitely no lightning inside the house!"

"Then what should we do?" Luna asked with a gasp.

"Let me make some coffee," I said, admitting defeat at last. It was clear that neither cat would let me go to bed until I found a way to bust this newborn ghost... or at least to send it off to haunt some place far, far away from here.

2

Coffee in hand, I settled myself at the kitchen table. The hard wood of the old chair did little to make me comfortable, but it did help keep me awake.

I took a slow sip from my mug, letting the steam warm my face, then glanced over at the two cats sitting across the table from me.

"So a ghost is coming," I said. "I can see how that would be a bad thing. Do either of you know how to make it go away?"

Luna shook her head sadly. "It's Virginia," she said, speaking of her late familiar. "I just know it is."

Merlin rubbed his head against his girlfriend's neck. "Her death wasn't your fault. It was her own greed."

"It feels like my fault," Luna mumbled. She'd been blaming herself ever since it happened. When she learned that Virginia had gone rogue in her thirst for magical power, Luna hadn't hesitated to sever the familiar bond, leaving them both powerless. And in her desperate grasp for the fleeing magic, Virginia toppled headfirst down a well and met her end.

Now apparently she was in the process of taking ghostly form and planning to haunt my house.

Was she after revenge?

Would she hurt me or one of the cats?

Whatever was going on, it definitely couldn't be good.

And just when I thought things were starting to settle down. *Ugh.*

My only hope now was that either the cats were wrong about the ghost or they had a different explanation for its presence.

I sucked in a deep breath, then let it out slowly. "I don't really know much about ghosts outside of what I've seen in old movies. Can one of you catch me up?"

Luna and Merlin exchanged a tense glance.

"What? What's wrong?" I asked with a heavy sigh. I almost didn't want to hear what they said next, but I needed to be prepared in case I found myself caught in the middle of another magical standoff.

Luna began to speak, but Merlin put the side of his paw against her chest to stop her.

"You're already distressed enough, my dear. Let me handle Gracie," he offered magnanimously.

"I don't like it when you talk about me as if I'm some kind of liability," I muttered as I wrapped both hands around my coffee mug to soak in its warmth.

"Look," said Merlin, approaching me slowly from across the table. "Luna and I are both young witches. Or, at least she was until... Anyway, the point is, I'm still a witch. A young one."

I groaned at his jumbled mix of explanatory stops and starts. I wish he could just tell it to me straight, no matter how bad. "Your point being?"

Merlin looked to Luna, who nodded for him to go on. He swallowed hard, then said,

"Well, neither of us has had any experience with ghosts before now, either."

I didn't understand their worry. So they didn't have practical experience. Book smarts could do in a pinch, and these two witchy cats seemed to have a limitless supply of knowledge when it came to the hidden world of magic.

When neither said more, I put on a smile. "No big deal. You learned how to deal with ghosts in witch school, right?"

A growl rumbled in Merlin's throat, and he lowered his eyelids as if it pained him to look at me. "Oh, you humans. So myopic in your world views. Just because you need years of schooling to function in society doesn't mean other creatures do. In fact, we witches learn much of what is needed simply by observing our everyday surroundings."

I scowled right back at him. I didn't get out of bed in the middle of the night just to be insulted by my feline roommates. "Great. And what's that taught you about ghosts?"

He coughed and looked away. "Fair point," he admitted. "I guess we aren't really equipped to deal with some of the rarer magical conundrums."

I drew in another slow, deep breath. "So where does that leave us? Do we just wait for the ghost to finish materializing and then ask it to leave?"

"Oh, no." Merlin scoffed. "Surely not."

"Ghosts are incredibly uncommon." Luna's voice was hardly more than a whisper from her side of the table. "The deceased only return to our world when they have a burning purpose. Something they wanted so badly while they were living that the quest for it became embedded in their very soul."

I shivered despite myself. "Sounds serious."

Merlin nodded. "To want something that much. It's often not good."

"Virginia yearned for power," Luna said softly. "The same thing that killed her could have brought her back."

"Yeah, that's definitely not good," I agreed, taking another long slurp from my coffee.

Both cats stared blankly at me while I drank. Somehow they treated me as a sidekick but then expected me to have all the answers.

"Um, can we capture it in a positronic box?" I suggested with a shrug. I hadn't seen Ghostbusters in a long time, but it was really the only frame of reference I had here. And somehow I doubted Virginia would be returning to us as a chubby green pizza-loving cartoon character.

"We don't deal in science," Merlin said with an exaggerated shudder. "This is a magic household, and you'll do well to remember that."

"To Nocturna then?" I asked, referencing the magical city that we could only enter at nightfall and with Merlin's aid.

Both cats nodded. "Nocturna."

3

As much as I wish I could've gone back to sleep, the coffee had done its job—meaning I was now up for the day. I had several hours to kill before my shift at the coffee shop, and I would have liked to tell you that I spent them working on my thesis research.

But, yeah, that's not what happened.

Instead of being productive, I whiled away the hours by watching the two Ghostbusters movies from the '80s. I didn't have time to get to the more recent adaptation but promised myself I'd watch it after work, Nocturna, and whatever other surprises managed to set my day off-kilter.

Of course, I got so absorbed in my mini movie marathon that I lost track of time and had to do my makeup in the car. My dark circles would now be on display to anyone who bothered to look at me for more than a few quick seconds.

Stupid ghost disturbing my sleep and messing up my look.

Even though I hoped our visit from that ghost was a one-off thing, I knew better than to expect a sound night's sleep anytime soon. That was the thing about the magical world—nothing was ever as easy as you'd hope. Even the two-blink teleport thing was full of problems and could kill somebody if not done properly.

Nope, not for me.

I'd stick to going places in my car, which was probably equally dangerous but at least more familiar, thank you very much.

Given an absence of red lights on my journey, I only managed to add a bit of eyeliner and a sassy matte lipstick before pulling into the parking lot at Harold's, but it would have to be enough.

My new boss Kelley Carmine insisted on

having her staff of baristas come into work, even though renovations kept the place closed to customers—and that felt odd to me.

Today, it seemed especially odd, seeing as our numbers had doubled. Before, only Drake, Kelley, and I had covered the majority of shifts, with the late Harold taking on whatever few we couldn't. When I arrived for work that day, though, three strangers stood huddled beside the brand-new espresso maker, watching as Kelley did the leg work for a round of pumpkin spice lattes.

That was her thing. While she'd kept the original name of the coffee shop to honor her late father, everything else about the business was undergoing a major transformation.

The most noticeable change was that every day was now pumpkin spice latte day. No longer could anyone order a simple latte, cappuccino, or Americano. Each now included at least some hint of pumpkin in the mix.

That was the hardest part of this transition for me, learning the new menu.

I fully supported Kelley's mission to offer PSL all year round, but that was before I realized the extent of her plans. We now had more than a dozen variants on the classic drink, including holiday versions that were also meant to be served year-round.

Want a cupid spice latte in August? No problem. We just need to add a shot of white chocolate and some red hot sprinkles to our classic PSL.

Blech. Just thinking of that monstrosity made my stomach churn.

"Welcome, Gracie!" my new boss cried with a giant grin on her eighteen-year-old face. "Now we just need Drake, and we can get started with the day you've all been waiting for!"

She paused as if she expected me to shout out some kind of answer. I didn't even know there'd been a question.

Kelley clucked her tongue. "C'mon, Gracie. You know better than anyone! It's one week until opening day, which means it's time to get everyone—including our lovely new hires—oriented to the new way of things. And..." She grabbed a pair of coffee stirrers and tapped them on the edge of the counter to imitate a drumroll. "That includes getting to taste everything on the menu! I hope you brought your appetites!"

How I managed not to throw up right then and there, I still don't know. Maybe Merlin's magic was starting to rub off on me, after all.

While I found Kelley's enthusiasm admirable, her commitment to the theme was just a bit too much for me. Still, I liked her and I wanted her to succeed. I also knew that no matter how far out into left field she went with this business, it was still destined to be a hit. I'd made sure of that when I secretly bestowed my one big wish upon her. Now I'd have to make my own destiny without any significant magical aid, and that was fine by me.

My life was exciting enough, thanks to my new adventures with Merlin and Luna... and our baby ghost. Plus I didn't trust myself not to waste the wish on something trivial—or something that would backfire on me spectacularly.

So Kelley got her PSL lovefest, and I got to keep my job. Let me tell you, the more things change, the more they just keep on staying the same.

4
———

Drake dragged himself through the door about ten minutes later, which made him eight minutes late for his shift. Harold would have torn him a new one—and then made him work at least an hour without pay. Kelley simply put on her best smile, clapped her hands together, and announced that we'd be starting off with an icebreaker.

She even climbed onto a chair and cupped her hands over her mouth like a megaphone—an action that was definitely not needed, given that we were all huddled closely together in the tiny storefront.

"My name is Kelley, and my favorite

pumpkin spice is ginger!" she shouted, then climbed down from the chair and motioned for me to climb up and take my turn.

I stumbled over, trying so hard not to be embarrassed as I rose up on that chair. "I'm Gracie, and I like cinnamon?" I said, having never really thought much about my favorite pumpkin spice before.

And so the day went, full of useless getting-to-know-you activities and overly sweet coffee confections. At one point, Kelley announced we'd be playing "Never have I ever" as her inventive, ice-breaking way of trying the new iced beverage line.

When it was my turn, I felt emboldened enough to say, "Never have I ever seen a ghost." It was kind of true. I knew there was a pre-ghost in my house, but only because my cats had told me.

What really surprised me was when Drake of all people kicked back his shot of pumpkin spice coconut dream.

Drake. Hmm. What did I know about Drake?

He had a bit of an attitude problem when it came to authority but had always been nice enough to me. The real question was whether he had taken a drink to be funny or if he'd actually seen a ghost. If he'd really come across one before, maybe he could help me with my problematic houseguest.

I had to find out, so I caught up with him in the parking lot as we were headed home from our mind-numbing afternoon of orientation activities.

"Hey, Drake," I called, jogging over to him. "Crazy day, huh?"

He shrugged casually with that same apathetic air he brought to everything. "It was pretty lame, but at least Kelley won't dock our pay like her old man did. That's something good, I guess."

I laughed, which made Drake raise one eyebrow and regard me with suspicion.

"Everything okay there, my PSL compadre?" he asked with a sly grin.

"Oh, yeah," I assured him, trying to ignore the heat that rose to my cheeks. "Just too much sugar today, I think."

He nodded and scooped his keys from his pocket. "Well, this is me." He motioned toward the shiny blue coupe we now stood beside. It was a much nicer car than I expected him to have. Seriously, how did he pay for this thing on his part-time barista salary?

"Okay, so bye, then," he said, when I remained silent for too long.

"Drake, wait!" I shouted before he could climb into the driver's seat and shut me out.

He settled on the seat but left the door wide open as he waited for me to tell him what I wanted.

I cleared my throat to buy a little time. This was an awkward question, especially if he'd been joking during our icebreaker. "I've been meaning to ask you—"

I didn't get to finish because he abruptly cut me off. "Yeah, sure I'll go out on a date with you," he answered, a debonair smile now on full display.

I blinked hard and took a step back. "Um, that's wasn't... Uh..." I had to make this right without alienating him so much that he'd refuse to share the details of his ghostly encounter. Unfortunately, this was a very new situation for me, and one I had a hard time putting into words. What were the rules of etiquette when it came to openly discussing the paranormal? And just how much could I share without risking my safety or freedom? Merlin had made it very clear that if I shared his witchy secret with non-magical folk, I would find myself locked away in a terrible supernatural prison for the rest of my life.

I was still debating how to frame my question when Drake spoke again.

"Your place at eight? Sounds awesome. I'll see you there."

And with that, he slammed the door shut and backed out of his spot, giving me one last mischievous look before he disappeared into traffic.

I jumped and waved my arms while shaking my head wildly, but I couldn't be sure that Drake caught sight of me in his rear-view mirror.

How had I messed this up so badly? I should have just blurted out my question. Trying to put things delicately had only made the whole situation worse.

Because now it seemed I had two problems on my hands.

And no idea how to solve either one.

5

I returned home to both cats sprawled out and sunning themselves on my kitchen floor. As they slept, their tails twitched with dreams. I hated to disturb them, especially given how adorable they looked relaxing together . Perhaps one day I'd have a relationship as gratifying as that of my cats, but today would not be that day. And that relationship would not be with Drake.

"We've got a problem," I announced as I pulled out a chair and sat to remove my shoes.

"Bigger than the ghost?" Merlin asked with a yawn.

"Not bigger, but a problem nonetheless."

"Let's hear it," Luna commanded after

she'd thoroughly stretched both her front and back legs and sauntered over to stand beside me.

"I kind of accidentally agreed, or maybe I invited... Um, I'm not sure how it happened, really, but I have a date with this guy from work." What was with me and words today? Why did I have such a hard time explaining even simple things? I must have done a poor job showing my displeasure, because both cats became very excited by my announcement.

"A date? That's fantastic." Luna's her blue eyes twinkled with glee. She sat taller and said, "Merlin and I have been worried about your love life lately."

"Seriously? It's only been like a week since you moved in here, Luna. How could you already be worried about my love life?" And was I really such a sad case that even my cats took pity on me? Cats famously didn't care what anyone thought about them, so why were they taking so much time thinking—and worrying—about me?

"Oh, a life without love is no life at all," Luna corrected me with a sigh. "Welcome to the living, Gracie."

"No, stop it." I hissed. Lately I'd been taking on more and more cat mannerisms, thanks to the influence of these two. The next thing I knew, I'd be licking the back of my hand and rubbing it across my forehead. God help me.

"This is not a real date," I continued, laying my displeasure on full display now. "It happened by accident, and he's coming over here tonight."

"But we're going to Nocturna tonight," Merlin reminded me, his whiskers twitching with newfound irritation.

"I know!" I shouted. Why was this so hard for them to understand?

"Then call and reschedule, dear," Luna suggested with a condescending air. I did not like this look on her. Or on me for that matter.

"I can't. I don't have his number."

Luna worked hard to maintain her smile, but even I could see it was faltering. "Then pay him a quick visit."

"I don't know where he lives."

"Then how does he know where you live, dear?" she asked with a sigh.

"That is a good question."

"You don't seem very excited for your date,"

she pointed out with a frown. "How did all this come about?"

I caught them up on all the ice-breaking activities and Drake's admission during "Never have I ever."

"That's a strange game. Why would humans want to brag about the things they haven't done? We cats like to share our accomplishments, not lack thereof," Merlin groused.

"The game is not the point," I snapped. "The point is that Drake has seen a ghost. And when I tried to ask him about that, it turned into this whole date thing."

"Well, a date is a perfect opportunity to ask him about his ghost, dear." Ah, Luna. Ever the optimist. It was starting to wear on me.

"Except we're supposed to be going to Nocturna tonight," I reminded them.

"You don't have to go everywhere we go," Merlin said rather grumpily. "If you want to abandon us in favor of your date, we'll live."

The beginnings of a tension headache crept up my neck and into my brain. Would it be wrong to turn a spray bottle on my cats to discipline them, knowing they could talk and that at least one of them could retaliate by conjuring lightning?

I tried very hard not to shout at the top of my lungs now. "That's not—"

Luna gently patted my hand with her paw. "It's fine, dear. Merlin and I will enjoy the alone time. We wouldn't want to be all up in your hair during your date, anyway."

"It's not—*UGH!*" This time I threw both hands in the air, then slammed them down on the table in frustration.

"So touchy," Merlin said with a sneer. "Don't worry, though, your highness. We'll do all the actual work that's needed to keep our home safe while you have fun entertaining your gentleman caller."

"You know what? Fine. Go to Nocturna. Have all the fun without me while I stay here and participate in a date I didn't ask for and don't want."

"Wonderful," Luna cooed. "So we're all in agreement then?"

I dropped my head into my hands and tried to focus on my breathing.

"Humans mature so much more slowly than cats," I heard Merlin whisper to Luna.

"Perhaps I'd have been better off with the old lady."

"Is it too late to switch?" the femme feline wondered aloud.

"You know better than anyone that once the familiar bond is set, it can't be broken without—"

Luna drew in a sharp breath. "Yes, I know."

"So we're stuck with her," he added glumly.

"I can still hear you!" I shouted, then stalked off to my room and slammed the door.

Hmm. Maybe they were right about my maturity level, after all.

6

The sun was due to set about fifteen minutes before eight o'clock that night, which meant that if Drake arrived even a few minutes early, he'd see my cat's magic on full display right in the front yard.

"Maybe we should consider moving your cauldron around back," I suggested as Merlin and Luna were making the final preparations for their journey to Nocturna. What I wouldn't give to go with them instead of having to stay here and entertain Drake in what would surely be an awkward encounter.

"Are you serious?" Merlin hissed, his eyes turning sharp. "If we move the cauldron, we may damage it. If we damage it, our connection to the magical world could be lost for good."

"Okay, okay, sorry," I muttered, kicking at a patch of extra-long grass near the driveway. As much as I loved being a homeowner now, I hadn't quite gotten the hang of the lawnmower yet. Every time I fired the thing up, the smell of freshly cut grass aggravated my allergies and sent me into a violent sneezing fit. But because the grass had to be cut one way or another, I end up running the mower back and forth over the yard as fast as I can, not bothering to make sure it gets cut evenly. Mostly cut was better than not cut at all, I figured, and since I didn't have the money to hire the job out, my neighbors would just have to deal with my uneven lawn.

"Next time, perhaps schedule your romantic tryst elsewhere," Luna purred. She began to rub against my leg, but I leapt out of reach. I was still not okay with the way she was treating me when it came to this accidental date—or to my love life at all.

"Not a romantic tryst. Not a romantic anything," I corrected between clenched teeth. "Remember, he invited himself over."

Merlin whispered something to Luna, just quietly enough that I couldn't make out the words. When he finished, they both turned toward me and began laughing.

"Just go to Nocturna already," I seethed, kicking another patch of mis-mown grass. "Stay there forever for all I care."

The cats continued to titter as they hopped into the birdbath, splashed around, and then disappeared in a glowing swirl of green. I doubted I'd ever get used to Merlin's strange modes of travel, either by turning his cauldron disguised as a bird bath into a portal or by blinking twice to magically teleport.

Every time my new life as a familiar began to make even a little bit of sense, something so bonkers came along I didn't think I'd ever be able to reconcile it with my previous understanding of the world.

I guess that was true of most things these days. Everything teetered somewhere between boring and safe or fascinating but stressful. I could pretty much guarantee that my life with Merlin would always fall into the latter category.

Now that he and Luna were gone, I had a

little while to play with my makeup, provided Drake arrived exactly on time or even a little bit late. Given his work history, I was banking on him being late, which meant I had some time to work on my look.

I hadn't dared lift a cosmetic brush or poof to my face while the cats were here teasing me. Still, whether or not I had asked for this date, I wanted to look nice. And I'd take any excuse to trot out one of my bolder makeup looks, really.

I didn't have any real dates happening in the near future, so I might as well use this fake date to try out the mermaid eyeshadow palate I'd purchased from a popular online boutique.

I worked fast to apply the array of bright colors, but not fast enough apparently, because the doorbell rang about halfway through my application.

"Coming," I called, turning my head slightly from side to side. If only I had another five minutes. *Grrr.*

Exactly on time, I noted with a quick glance at the microwave clock as I passed through the kitchen. Definitely not what I'd expected from Drake.

I found him waiting patiently on my

doorstep, wearing a black dress shirt, tie, and suit jacket with jeans and a pair of ordinary, scuffed-up sneakers.

"Hi, Drake," I said, my eyes landing on the single flower he held clutched within his hand. The bloom was a deep blood red with spiky looking petals, definitely not something I recognized.

"For you," he said with a small smile that I found almost charming.

"Thank you," I said, accepting the gift. "It's really pretty."

"That's a black narcissus, a cactus Dahlia," he explained in that smug way of his.

"I don't know much about flowers," I admitted with a slight frown. "Cactuses don't need water, right?"

"Cacti is the plural of cactus," he corrected with a chuckle, shoving both hands into his pockets now. "And the flower has already been cut. It will die, no matter what you do with it now. So go nuts."

"Oh," I said for lack of a better response to his unsettling instructions. "Well, thanks again. I guess you should come on in."

I hurried to the kitchen to find something

to put my flower in. Surely, Grandma Grace had left a vase or two somewhere in here. In the end, I gave up searching and simply placed it in an empty pitcher that I'd used once or twice to make lemonade.

Drake definitely got points for bringing me a flower, I'd give him that. But since this wasn't an actual date, the points didn't matter a lick.

Come to think of it, I hadn't gone on a date since relocating to Elderberry Heights, nor had I wanted to go on one. At first, I'd been too busy settling into my new house and job while still pretending to make forward progress on my thesis. And now I was too busy solving murders, fighting mad mages, and corralling talking cats. At this rate, I'd be lucky to ever go on a real date again.

But Drake didn't need to know any of that.

I had one mission here and one mission alone—find out what he knew about ghosts and see if it could help with my little situation.

7

"So is this a Netflix and chill situation, or...?" Drake raised an eyebrow and smiled at me suggestively.

I couldn't suppress the shudder that wracked through me at that thought. "Eww, no. Just give me five minutes and then I'll be ready to go out."

"Go where?" he asked, following me toward the hall.

"I don't know. Wherever you want," I called over my shoulder before stepping inside the bathroom and closing the door.

"You're the one who asked me out," he shouted from the other side. "I assumed you had a plan."

I bit my lip to keep myself from giving it to him straight. If I ranted about how I'd never meant to invite him on this so-called date, he probably wouldn't be up to sharing what he knew about ghosts. So for now, I'd just have to play along.

"How about a moonlit walk?" I suggested once I emerged from the bathroom, my look now complete. That at least put me in a better mood.

"Pretty eyes," Drake said with an approving nod. "I like that look on you."

"You know about makeup?" I squeaked.

"Not much, but I make it my business to know a little bit about a lot of things. Keeps life interesting. And, sure, I could go for a walk." He grinned and motioned for me to lead the way.

Suddenly I felt nervous.

Drake clearly paid a lot better attention to his surroundings than I previously gave him credit for. Did that mean I'd given off some kind of vibe suggesting I wanted to date him?

Outside, Drake offered me the crook of his arm, and I looped mine through, feeling extra fancy as we strolled through the neighborhood.

"So how'd you get into the bean business?" he asked as he kept his eyes fixed on the distant horizon.

"Putting myself through graduate school," I answered by rote. His was a question I'd answered often, especially when my professors and fellow students asked why I was distracting myself with this temporary job when I could simply finish my degree and find a much better gig. "How about you?"

"Just following orders." He flashed me an impish grin.

"What? Whose orders?"

He let out a fatigued sigh. "It's a condition of my trust fund. I have to keep a steady job to collect. So just to stick it to my old man, I keep the lowliest job possible, doing the exact opposite of what he'd intended for me."

"So you're a trust fund baby? That explains a few things," I said, thinking back to his shiny sports coupe.

"Darling, I'm a trust fund man, and don't you forget it." He smiled charmingly, and I couldn't help but laugh. This was something we had in common, at least. The people in our lives expected more of us—or rather different things. I knew I'd finish my degree eventually, but I still had no idea what I actually wanted for my life. In truth, I'd chosen Sociology as my field of study because it seemed to be one of the broadest majors available. I'd then signed on to grad school because that's what you were supposed to do when your bachelor's degree didn't offer a clear career path.

I still preferred that life be full of surprises, and settling into a 9-to-5 felt like the exact opposite of that.

"Don't you get bored, though?" I asked Drake now. "With only working part-time and having no aspirations outside of continuing to collect?" He didn't need to know that my own aspirations were as of yet undefined.

"Bored? No way. And who says I don't have aspirations. Like I said, I like to know a little bit about a lot of things. A modern renaissance man."

"Like gardening," I supplied with a slight grin. "And makeup."

He nodded. "And ghosts."

Oh, good. He'd given me the lead in I needed. I jumped for it. "Actually, I was wondering about that."

He hung his head and laughed. "Of course, you were. You don't think I knew that in the parking lot?"

I stopped walking and stared after him. "But you—"

He also stopped a few paces ahead and then turned to study me. "I turned the situation to my advantage. I've been wanting to take you out for a long time. I figured this way you'd want it, too."

"Sneaky." Now my smile was so big it was busting at the seams.

He winked at me. "Or genius."

"I'll stick with sneaky," I answered with a laugh, then began walking again and looped my arm through his once more. "So are you going to tell me about the ghosts?"

"Ghost," he corrected. His smile had been replaced by a clenched jaw and furrowed brow. "I've only ever seen the one."

"Tell me about it," I practically begged as I gave his forearm a little squeeze.

His expression lightened again. "Well, I

guess I got what I wanted out of tonight—that is, some extra time with you. I suppose it's only fair to give you what you wanted. One ghost story coming right up."

He cleared his throat to begin...

8

"Okay, so it was a dark and stormy night..."

I groaned and flung my head back dramatically. "Seriously?"

"If you want the story, then you've gotta let me set the scene," Drake said, his dark hair falling into his eyes as he smiled at me from just one side of his mouth.

I rolled my eyes and motioned for him to go ahead.

"Like I was saying, it was a dark and stormy night." He widened his eyes and glared at me, daring me to protest.

When I kept mum, he smiled with the other half of his mouth, too.

"I'd just turned twenty-one, which meant I'd finally come into my trust fund, and now I was in the process of driving all over the country in search of a new place to settle down. The only requirement? That it be as far away from my parents as possible. I was on my way to Miami when a giant storm whipped up, so I pulled over to the side of the road to wait it out. While I sat there, this lady in white appeared out of nowhere." His eyes became vacant as he journeyed deeper into the memory, and I had no doubt he was seeing the scene unfold anew in his mind's eye.

Drake took a deep, stuttering breath before continuing. "She wore this old-fashioned gown and no shoes. I could barely see her through the thick sheet of rain, but it was enough to tell that she was semi-transparent."

I gasped. "Wow, you really did see a ghost."

"Why would I lie about it?" he asked with one dark eyebrow raised in question.

The intensity of his gaze made me let go of his arm and take a small step to the side. "You're right. I'm sorry. Go ahead."

He shrugged. "There's not much else to tell. Another car showed up, almost drove straight into the thing, but then skidded off road at the very last minute. A soccer mom van stopped to help the person who'd crashed. Eventually the rain stopped, and I carried on toward Miami. Stayed there for a few months but got sick of all the sun. I came back up to Georgia, looking for the place I'd seen the ghost. Eventually I gave up my search. That was when I saw the help wanted sign at Harold's and decided to settle in Elderberry Heights."

"Wow," I whispered in awe, even though I had yet to process his story in its entirety. "So you definitely believe in ghosts?"

"Definitely," he declared unequivocally as if he'd been asked whether the sky was blue. "I've toured haunted houses and talked to psychic mediums in the time since, but everyone I've found has been a fraud."

I grabbed him by the shoulder and waited for him to bend down so I could whisper, "What if I told you I had a ghost materializing in my house right now?"

Drake's eyes lit up with intrigue. "Then I'd ask what we're doing out here. Can I see it? Can I talk to it?" He looked like a kid at Christmas.

"I'm not sure it can talk yet, but I know it's there. Weak, but seems to be getting stronger." I was proud of myself for not mentioning the cats in my explanation.

I worried that he'd ask questions I didn't know how to answer, but instead he whipped around and began walking quickly back toward my house, so eager he was to see this ghost for himself.

"That's my biggest regret, you know," he said as I struggled to match his pace. "That I just sat in my car the whole time rather than getting out and trying to communicate with it."

"But you said that a car ran it through," I reminded him, wrapping my arms around my torso as we walked. Even though it wasn't the slightest bit cold out, I still needed that added bit of comfort to counteract how this conversation had started making me feel.

He nodded. "Yes, another car scared it off, but there were several minutes of the spirit just floating there. It seemed like maybe she was waiting for someone or something."

This was getting creepy. I mean, it had already started pretty creepily, but the more Drake shared of his otherworldly experience, the more I began to worry about how my own might play out.

Could my house ghost even be scared off? And if I tried too hard to get rid of it, could the cats and I end up missing an important message from the other side?

If only I knew...

9

I led Drake back to my house and invited him inside to meet my baby ghost. I felt much better allowing him in this time. He now knew where we stood as far as this evening's non-date, and he'd already confided in me with his ghostly experience.

Granted, I still hoped he'd clear out before the cats returned from Nocturna. I didn't think I could endure another merciless round of their teasing.

"Well? Where is it?" he asked eagerly, glancing all around the house as if he'd be able to see it with his naked eyes.

"I'm not sure it's out yet. I think it's strongest at night, and the sun has only just gone down," I explained as I pointed to the top corner of the narrow hallway leading to my bedroom.

Drake marched right over to the spot I'd pointed out and reached up a hand with outstretched fingers.

"What are you doing?" I guffawed, resisting the urge to slap my palm into my forehead. "Trying to give the thing a high five?"

He turned back toward me and made a face, not embarrassed as I'd expect but more playful. "I'm checking to see if there's a temporal anomaly."

I chuffed at this. "And? Is there?"

"Well, I just realized that I have no idea what a temporal anomaly would feel like. Yeah, I've seen a ghost before, but that was more dumb luck than anything." He tilted his head to the side. "How did you know it was here?"

My heart thudded in my chest. I hated lying, but telling him the truth about Merlin would result in me being locked away in some dodgy magical prison for the rest of my life. That one simple fact made lying essential, but it didn't make me good at it.

"Oh, it's my, uh, intuition," I hedged.

"Sometimes I can hear things other people can't." That was true, if only because the cats chose to talk to me instead of most other humans.

His eyes widened, and he seemed to look at me with a fresh perspective. "Whoa. So you actually heard it, then? Did it speak to you, like in words?"

I shook my head quickly. "No, no words. It's more like the sound of, uh, waves crashing softly on the beach."

"How does one crash softly?" he asked with a chuckle.

I couldn't tell whether that was a rhetorical question, so I chanced an answer. "It's hard to explain. Like *shhspspspspshh.*"

"Sounds like how some people call their cats," he pointed out with another soft laugh.

I smiled awkwardly. "Haha, yeah, it kind of does. Anyway, maybe I'm panicking over nothing. I mean, it all sounds pretty crazy, right?"

Drake walked back toward me at the other end of the hall. "Crazy is just what people like to call things they don't quite understand. For what it's worth, I believe you about your ghost, and I think it's pretty freaking cool."

"Thanks," I said with a sigh of relief.

Drake raised his hand to touch my forearm. "You're pretty freaking cool, Gracie. There's something different about you. Especially lately. And, well, I really, really like it."

I swallowed hard. "Th-thank you."

His eyes softened around the edges as he ran his palm up my arm. "Look," he murmured. "I know I backed you into this date, and that you were too nice to say no. But you can say no now. Okay?"

I nodded as his hand finally reached my shoulder.

He took another step forward. "May I kiss you?"

Oh, wow. That came out of nowhere. "No!" I said, perhaps a bit too emphatically.

Drake immediately dropped his hand and took a step back. He wore a smile, but it was definitely forced.

"I'm sorry," I mumbled. "It's just that I have a lot going on in my life right now, and—"

Drake held up a palm. "It's okay. I get it. I didn't think you were into me, but I had to find out for sure. I'll leave you to your evening. If you need any more help with your ghost or just want to hang out, you know where to find me."

He moved past me and made a beeline for the door.

"Drake, I'm sorry!" I called before rushing after him. "I do like you, and I've enjoyed hanging out with you tonight. But I just don't know you that well yet. And the part about having too much going on to make space for a relationship. That's one-hundred percent true."

He tilted his head slightly to the side. "You don't have to explain it to me. I'm definitely an acquired taste."

"Hey, then maybe I'll acquire it after we spend more time together," I blurted out stupidly. I didn't feel that way about Drake, and I wasn't sure I ever could.

He paused with his hand on the doorknob. "So you think you might get a craving for some vitamin D later?"

My mouth fell open. I tried to issue a response, but it came out as more of a disgusted groan.

Drake spun around to face me. "D for Drake! That's all I meant! D for Drake. Not... the other thing."

I nodded mutely, my eyes still wide from shock.

"Yeah, I'll just go jump off a bridge now," he said, pulling the door open and stepping outside.

For a moment, I debated going after him, but then—

10

"Out of my way, out of my way!" Merlin yowled as he and Luna popped out from the birdbath in a cascade of green sparks.

"Hush, or someone will see you!" I whisper-yelled from my spot in the doorway. I glanced toward the road and was relieved to see that Drake had made his getaway before the magical display on my front lawn.

"That was a close one," Merlin muttered as he and Luna passed by me on their way inside the house.

I shut the door and locked it. Just in case.

"What happened?" I asked, almost afraid to hear their answer.

Luna stretched to lick Merlin's forehead,

and he visibly let go of some of the tension he'd carried home with him.

"Thanks. I needed that," he purred to his lady love while continuing to ignore me.

Luna attached herself to Merlin's side. I wouldn't have been able to pry them apart if I tried. And I definitely knew better than to try.

"We ran into some cats from Merlin's past, and they weren't exactly happy to see him. Or to see us together," she explained in that lilting voice of hers.

"What did they do?" I asked. Merlin was hardly more than a kitten. Him taking me on as his familiar was the act that officially made him a full-fledged witch, and that had happened very recently. How could such a young cat already have such bitter enemies?

"They challenged him to a duel, which he —" She narrowed her eyes at Merlin. "—then foolishly accepted."

"Whoa, you could have died tonight?" I spat with equal parts surprise and anxiety. "What were you thinking?"

"He wasn't thinking," Luna answered with a sigh. "But you must also remember that we cats do things differently than humans."

"Duels with guns, right? Like in Hamilton?" I pictured Merlin wearing a period costume and circling another cat in colonial garb while they rapped about their grievances. Now there's a show I would pay good money to see.

"Certainly not," Luna said, her lip curled in disgust, almost as if she'd been able to picture the scene playing out in my head.

"Then?" I asked seriously.

Merlin spoke up at last, his fur twitching at the shoulders. "It wouldn't have been so bad. We cats fight with what's at our disposal."

He raised a paw and unsheathed his claws. "We use a combination of magic and good-old fashioned rough-housing."

Luna nudged him until he put his weapons away. "Cats strike with their paws. Magical cats strike with phantom claws."

I shook my head, not understanding the strange metaphor.

"We bat at each other's magic within," he explained, then pressed his ears back against his head, raised a paw, and hit at the air. "Like that, but we don't aim to injure faces or hurt pride. We attack each other's magic until one of us doesn't have enough left to continue the duel."

"You kill each other?" The thought seemed so barbaric. But I guess if humans could take each other's lives, then so, too, could other species. As much as I wished they wouldn't.

Merlin shuddered. "No, it's much worse. The loser lives on without magic. A fate worse than—"

"Ah-ah-ahem!" I cleared my throat loudly to stop him.

"What's your problem?" Merlin asked, then glanced to Luna at his side and dipped his head in regret. "Oh, right. Sorry."

"I know you didn't mean it," she said softly, still clearly hurt by his words. "Just as I know you wouldn't want to risk your magic when we have an imminent threat in our own home."

"Why did those other cats even want to fight you? Surely, nothing you've done could have been *that* bad." Sometimes he was sarcastic and off-putting, but overall, Merlin was a good cat. He didn't seem like the enemy type... Well, other than that thing with Luna. Actually, you know what? Never mind. He'd clearly made his fair share of enemies in his short life. Maybe that was just the way with magic. I was still new to this world and learning all its quirks.

Merlin growled. "Well, before Luna was my girl, she was Tom's."

"Tom," I repeated. "Tom Cat?"

"Yes, and when he saw her without magic, he blamed me. Tom became so angry, he challenged me as part of some misguided attempt to avenge her."

"That's actually kind of sweet," I said with a sappy smile.

Luna shook her head adamantly. "I do not need to be avenged by Merlin, Tom, or anyone else. I make my own choices, and I fight my own battles with or without magic. Of course, Merlin agreed to the duel before I had a chance to tell him any of this."

Merlin nodded somberly. "And when Luna made her displeasure known, the only thing we could do was run and hope we made it back through the portal before Tom and his cronies could catch us."

"Please tell me you got what we needed regarding the ghost before all this went down," I mumbled, upset.

"Of course we did," Luna answered with a wide grin, which quickly faltered. "Although it would probably be best if Merlin doesn't show his face in Nocturna for a while."

"But without Merlin, neither of us can go."

"I know," she said with a flick of her tail. "So consider Nocturna off our resource list for the moment."

Great. Our direct connection to the magical world had been temporarily severed while we struggled to deal with a very real, very immediate magical problem.

That would make things so much easier.

11

"But you said you got what we needed," I pointed out, hoping very much that this was true. Without the ability to access other magical creatures in Nocturna, we'd be truly alone in dealing with our unwanted house ghost.

"Relax, will you?" Merlin spat as he stared at me with large green eyes. "Don't you remember rule one?"

Yes, I remembered that I was supposed to trust everything he said without question. A terrible rule, but one he insisted on enforcing.

I pressed my lips into a firm line and waited for him to share more.

And once he was satisfied with my quiet

compliance, he went ahead with his explanation. "We went to the library and found a spell we can use to trap the ghost."

My jaw dropped open. "Nocturna has a library?" I squealed with glee. Oh, how badly I now wanted to go.

"Yes. What's the big deal?" He wagged his tail wildly like one of those giant wavy men in front of an auto dealership.

"Nothing. I just love books, and—"

"Can we focus on what's important here?" Merlin snapped, clearly still out of sorts from his near duel with the rival Tom Cat.

Luna fixed me with a kindly gaze. "The library is lovely, but it is made for cats. I'm afraid you wouldn't fit through the door, dear."

Well, there was that dream dashed. I hadn't even been granted proper time to picture myself ensconced in stacks of magical old books. *Sigh.*

Merlin lay down in loaf form with his paws tucked beneath him, apparently now delegating the task of dealing with me to Luna.

She stood and stretched, keeping her tail high in the air. "We found the spell we need, and I should have all the ingredients for it in my garden. Since I am no longer magical, I won't be able to mix the potion myself, but I still have the knowledge. I can guide Merlin in its creation. Or even you."

Oh, that was right. As Merlin's familiar, I was also a vessel for his magic. Kind of like a portable battery charger. I couldn't cast any magic myself, but I always had a ready source for my feline overlord.

"One problem," I realized aloud. "Your garden is at Virginia's old place. We don't have access to it."

She grinned a devilish grin. "It's outside. All we have to do is walk up and take what we need."

I twisted my mouth in a grimace. "Isn't that stealing, though?"

Merlin laughed. "After all we've been through, you're worried about stealing? Besides, that garden is Luna's. She planted it, cared for it. How could it be anyone's but hers?"

"Don't think about it too hard. You'll just give yourself a headache," Luna suggested. She then pressed herself into Merlin's side. "Well, c'mon. We need to get those ingredients if we're to dispatch our ghost."

I sighed. She was right, of course. That didn't make me feel any better about sneaking around on a property that didn't belong to us. Just look at all the trouble it had gotten us into before!

Still, once the cats had made up their minds, there was no convincing them otherwise.

I placed a hand on the Maine Coon witch's back, resigned to what would happen next.

Merlin just had to blink twice, and the three of us were transported to the garden.

Well, actually, we ended up at the far edge of the yard near a thick tree that I knew all too well. I shivered, remembering the times I'd been here before. None of them had been pleasant. First Merlin and I had broken in, only to be threatened by our then-enemy, Luna. She also kidnapped me and used me to make a love spell, although I didn't know that at the time. The worst memory of all, though, was the showdown we had with Virginia and the wicked illusion witch who'd been pulling her strings. The same tree we found ourselves standing by now had been animated and fought right alongside us.

Creepy, creepy, creepy.

Was it any wonder I was so hesitant about returning now in the dead of night?

A flash of red caught my eye. I turned quickly, half expecting to see a crazed witch running right at me. But it was only the FOR SALE sign flapping in the gentle breeze.

Luna drew up to my side and said, "Virginia had no family. No next of kin. That's part of why I chose her. It's much easier to make a familiar of someone without attachments."

"Is that why you chose me?" I asked Merlin, wondering if I should be offended. Did the witchy cats choose people human society didn't want? Did this mean my cats thought I was a loser who wouldn't be missed?

"That's why I chose your grandmother," Merlin explained without looking my way. "I chose you by default when she left."

I chuffed. "Thanks for reminding me."

"Hey, I'm happy with my choice, however it was made."

That at least made me smile. "Okay, so we're here for ingredients, right? Let's get what we need and go. Whether or not anyone lives here now, I still don't feel right about snooping around."

"Your sense of morality is seriously questionable at times," Merlin said as he raised his head and sniffed the air. "But so be it."

12

Luna led the way into the back garden. I had a hard time seeing much in the darkness of night, but neither cat hesitated as they plucked various herbs and flowers from the ground and laid them in a pile at my unmoving feet.

"Are you almost done?" I asked after several minutes of this.

That was when a flood light lit up the backyard, blinding me in its sudden brightness.

"Hello!" someone called from the side of the house as footsteps hurried our way. "Who's out here?"

I froze in place, hoping Merlin would transport us out of there before the other person made it back.

No such luck, though. Honestly, I don't think he even tried.

"Gracie?" the other person shouted with a gasp. "What are you doing back here?"

Finally my eyes began to adjust to the light. I squinted at the new arrival and watched as it slowly morphed into the familiar shape of my friend and boss, Kelley Carmine.

"Hi," I said with an awkward wave.

"What are you doing here?" she asked, stepping closer without hesitation now that we'd identified each other.

"Oh, you know..." I laughed to disguise my nerves. "Taking my cats for a nice moonlit stroll."

She tilted her head to the side. "In my back garden?"

I took a step back. "Your garden? I thought this place was for sale. I'm sorry, I didn't realize—"

"Oh, you're fine." Kelley waved her hand dismissively and made a funny face. "It's not officially mine yet. My offer was accepted just today, though, which means it will be soon."

"Kelley, congrats! That's amazing!" I broke into a relieved smile. I didn't like snooping around my friend's place uninvited, but it was much better than if it were a stranger's.

Her cheeks reddened slightly. "Yeah, now that I own a business here, I'm trying to put down some roots. It felt weird to live in my dad's old place, so I did some searching and found this cute little cottage. I just came by to take some measurements so I can start planning."

"Well, you picked a nice house. This garden is very pretty."

We both looked toward the rows of herbs and flowers that filled almost half of the back yard.

Kelley shook her head. "Do you think so? I don't even know what half these plants are. I was actually thinking of tearing everything out and replacing it with tulips. That's my favorite flower, and I hear they're much easier to take care of than some others."

Luna gasped and fell over onto the grass.

"Um, is your cat okay?"

"Oh, yes. Luna's fine. They're both fine. Sorry about appearing unexpectedly like this.

The cats kind of lead the way, and I follow." This was the best misdirect I'd come up with yet, because it was totally true—just not in the current context.

"That's okay. Like I said, it's not mine yet. But when it is, you and your cats will be welcome anytime." Kelley then grabbed my hand and tugged me along after her. "Since you're here, you might as well come in and see it. Can you believe it, Gracie? I just bought an entire house! Or I guess I'm about to, but still! A house!"

I laughed as we made our way toward the front door together. While it was strange that Kelley had purchased this exact house, I wasn't the least bit surprised she was soon to be a homeowner. Her father would have been so proud.

I, however, couldn't let her know that I'd already been inside because then I'd have to come up with lies to explain myself.

Kelley fiddled with the Realtor's lockbox on the door and extracted a key. "You have to use your imagination a little, okay? The previous owner had terrible taste, but my agent assures me that everything will be cleared out of here well before I move in."

I smiled and nodded as she fitted the key into the lock above the doorknob.

"That's a lot of floral print," I exclaimed as soon as she flicked on the lights. Of course it was a lot of floral print—this place had been inhabited by a garden witch and her familiar.

"It's kind of sad, isn't it? I don't know how the previous owner died, but I know she had nobody to claim this house or any of her things. When I think of her, I picture this poor little old lady locked up in this time capsule of a house with only a cat or two to keep her company." She glanced over at me and worried her lip. "No offense."

Boy, had she gotten Virginia wrong.

"No offense about the cats?" I asked with a playful grin.

"About your house. I didn't mean to imply that retro can't be cool. It's just—" She motioned around the room. "There's so much floral in here."

Well now, apparently I'd become an old lady stereotype. *Fabulous.*

"My house belonged to my grandma," I

explained as we both strode toward the kitchen. "I have lots of good memories that happened inside that house exactly as it is. I don't have the heart to change it."

Kelley's face immediately crumpled into a frown. "Oh, I'm so sorry. I didn't realize... My condolences."

I chuckled. "Grandma Grace isn't dead. She's just in Florida."

"Well, that's good, I suppose." She winked at me, then guided me into the small formal dining room. "Someday I'll have you and the others from work over for a real sit-down dinner party."

"Sounds great," I enthused.

"Oh, it will be," she promised, her eyes practically glazing over as if she were seeing that future scene before her.

I, however, couldn't see past Virginia and the horrible events that occurred here.

Well, at least I knew Virginia was haunting me and would probably leave Kelley alone. Because as hard as it might be to protect myself from an angry spirit, I imagined it would be even harder to help a friend without revealing the existence of magic.

13

After showing me the master suite, Kelley walked me back out into the hall and turned to me with worry reflecting in her pale eyes. "Gracie, do you think I'm taking on too much at once? With the coffee shop and now this house? I mean, I've hardly been in town for a month and, well, I'm kind of in a vulnerable spot, what with meeting my dad and then losing him, and—"

I placed a hand on her shoulder. "Kelley, it's okay. It is a lot, but you've got this. You've already made such amazing progress with the coffeehouse, and you'll do great things with this house, too."

She blinked up at me with glistening eyes. "Do you mean it?"

"Of course I do. I believe in you, and I'll be with you every step of the way." It seemed I'd accidentally become Kelley's mentor by helping her through her father's death. That was okay, though. I really liked her and wanted her to be happy. I also hoped she never found out that I had initially suspected her of murdering her dad. I now knew she would never do such an awful thing. She just didn't have it in her.

Kelley sighed and offered me a tight hug. "I'm so lucky to have a friend like you. Seriously. It's like there's this vice around my chest. And as we move closer and closer to the grand re-opening, it tightens a little each day. It's already getting hard to breathe now. What will it be like when the big day is finally here? I worry that I won't have any oxygen left."

I patted the back of her head like one would do with an upset child. In truth, Kelley was little more than a child. She had an awful lot on her plate for an eighteen-year-old. Even though I was still pretty young myself, I had nowhere near as many responsibilities thrust upon me—that is, if you chose to ignore the whole magical cat with a seemingly unending supply of enemies.

"It's anxiety," I told her, recalling something my grandma had once told me. "It may seem like a bad thing, but it's good, too."

Kelley pulled back and looked at me like I was crazy. "A good thing? How?"

"It means you care. Life is so much better when you have things and people that matter to you. And the best part? You can harness that anxiety as motivation. Fuel. Use that nervous energy to propel you toward your goal, and you'll be there in no time."

"Seems like you speak from experience," she said with a tight smile.

I nodded. "Well, from my grandma's, at least."

"It's good advice. Did your grandma have anything to say about love?"

I widened my eyes at this. "Love!"

My friend turned bright red and looked toward the floor. "Well, it's a crush, and I know I have no extra time to think about things like this, but every time I see him come into the coffee shop, I— Oops, I've said too much."

"Kelley!" I gasped, grabbing her forearm and forcing her to look up at me. "Please tell me it's not Drake."

She shrugged coyly. "I know, I know. He's just so cool, like he doesn't care what anyone thinks of him. I wish I had that kind of confidence."

"It's important to you what others think, and that's okay. It's because you care about them. That's way better than Drake's cool confidence."

"Maybe, but he's just so smart, and he has all this random knowledge."

"He knows a little bit about a lot of things," I said, recalling his words from earlier that night.

"Exactly!" Kelley crooned. "Do you think I've got a shot with him?"

"Well, you're kind of his boss. I'm pretty sure there's laws against that kind of thing."

Her features pinched into a frown. "You're right. What was I thinking? I don't have time for a relationship right now anyway."

"Hey. There will be time for all that later. And you're going to make some guy very happy one day. Look at you with the business and the house!" I hated to discourage her, but I also knew that Drake was interested in someone else—me. What I would give for that not to be true, especially now that I knew Kelley would happily take my place as the object of his affection.

She smiled. "You're right about that, too. I should probably let you get back to your cats before they run away on you, huh?"

Right, the cats.

I gave her another quick hug. "Thanks for showing me around. It's a lovely house. Congrats again, Kelley, and see you at work!"

I let myself out and raced back around the house, using my phone light to guide me. I found both cats standing near the old well that had served as Luna's cauldron.

Luna had a lovesick expression on her face, and Merlin was the very picture of rage. Had I just walked in on my cats canoodling? *Really?*

"If you two have kittens, I am not raising them!" I growled into the night.

"That's enough out of you," Merlin growled right back. "It's not our fault you took forever in there. We had to do something to pass the time. Now are we ready to go, your highness?"

I nodded stupidly.

"Then lay your hand on me, and I'll teleport us back home," the cat commanded.

I hesitated. "Um, that's okay."

Luna stepped forward, her blue eyes taking on a red hue in my flashlight. "Gracie, dear. I know what you're thinking, and it's all right. We were only grooming each other."

Grooming, uh-huh.

Still, I didn't want to stay stuck in this awkward situation any longer than I had to. I placed a hand on Merlin's head.

He blinked twice, and we were home.

14

"Wait," I cried as my feet touched down on the linoleum kitchen floor. "We forgot the ingredients for the spell!"

"Already took care of that while we were waiting," Merlin said, jerking his head toward the table where an array of plant life had been spread across the surface.

"What's this for?" I asked, picking up the only non-organic object on the table—a ceramic garden decoration shaped like a frog with a giant, open mouth.

Luna smiled wistfully. "This was Virginia's. It used to sit on the edge of the porch. She used it to hide her spare house key."

"Yeah, her and everyone else in the state of Georgia," I quipped. Seriously, why have a spare key at all if you were going to make its hiding spot so obvious? "Why did you bring it back? Are you missing her, Luna?"

The normally docile cat snarled at me. "Heavens no! Why would you even think I'd miss that monster? We need something that belonged to the spirit in life. It will help us summon and trap her."

"As opposed to some other ghost?" I deadpanned. "Because we have so many ghosts knocking on our door."

Luna shook her head at my snippiness. "The potency of any spell is much stronger if you add an object that belongs or belonged to the intended recipient."

Oh, yes. I knew this. "Like when you took Merlin's hair for the love spell?" I pointed out with one eyebrow raised.

She let out a little cough. "Precisely."

"So is everything ready? Can we make the potion now?"

"Carry it outside for us, and we can get started," the she-cat told me, and I was quick to comply.

Once again, though, I questioned the wisdom of keeping the cauldron in our front yard, but it was at least late enough that we probably wouldn't need to worry about gawking neighbors.

The cats worked together in mixing the brew while I kept my eyes on the street, just in case I needed to sound the alarm.

Thankfully, it only took a few minutes for them to finish their witchy work.

"Gracie, come grab this," Luna called when they were done.

Inside the bird bath sat the little ceramic frog, its mouth filled with a dark green liquid. It looked like one of those disgusting concoctions my mother used to make in her juicer and then try to force me to drink in the mornings before school.

I didn't care that it had antioxidants, I refused to ingest something that looked like it had been scraped from the bottom of a pond—and smelled that way, too.

I could hardly suppress a gag as I lifted the frog full of potion and carried it into the house.

"Put it in the hallway near the back corner,"

Luna instructed. "The same place we sensed the ghost forming last night."

"Remind me what this will do," I said after following her instructions to the letter.

"It will help Virginia to materialize faster, and then it will trap her in place so we can deal with her."

"And how do we plan to deal with her?"

"Eh, we'll figure it out when the time comes," Merlin added with a long, lazy stretch.

"Wonderful," I muttered, pouring some crunches into the cats' bowl for them. "So glad to know we're doing everything we can to make sure we stay safe. Now if you don't need me any longer, I'm going to bed."

Both cats raced over to eat. Before lowering his head to the bowl, though, Merlin glanced over to the counter and frowned. "Luna, my love, did we forget one of the ingredients for our potion tonight?"

She stopped eating and raised her head. "No. Everything that should have been included was."

"Then what's that?" he asked, pointing his nose toward the counter where the black cactus dahlia Drake had given me still sat in a half-empty glass pitcher.

Both cats glanced toward the counter and then me.

"Gracie," Luna prattled in a sing-song voice. "That's not from my garden. Does it belong to you?"

No, no, no. I had hoped we'd all been busy enough that we could just skip past the part where the cats teased me about my non-date. They'd already laid into me pretty hard before Drake came over, and I just didn't have the energy to endure their teasing a second time.

"It was a gift. Don't worry about it," I said, crossing my arms over my chest.

"From your new boyfriend?" Luna cooed, her tail waving from side to side in delight.

"What was his name again?" Merlin asked, kicking up his back leg to scratch behind his ear.

"Drake," Luna answered promptly.

"Not my boyfriend. Not even close," I said through clenched teeth.

"But he gave you a flower," Luna pointed out. "Isn't that considered a romantic gesture among humans?"

"Yeah, he wants me. I don't want him. In fact, my other friend does. Ugh, never mind. Can we just move past this whole elementary school thing, please?"

"What's elementary school?" they both asked, completely transfixed on me now.

"It's a place human kids go when they're like six."

"I'm only one year old," Merlin said with a shrug.

"Me, too," Luna chimed.

"So I guess it's not past us then," Merlin said with a sinister smile. "Now tell us, did Drakey Wakey kiss you nighty wighty?"

"I'm going to bed!" I shouted, then stomped off and slammed my bedroom door for the second time that day.

15

I woke up the next morning to bright rays of sunlight shooting through my blinds. Ugh. I really needed to invest in some black-out curtains if I ever wanted to sleep past sunrise again.

After a quick pit stop to the bathroom, I trudged into the kitchen and straight to my favorite appliance, then popped in a dark roast pod and waited for it to brew.

My morning coffee was becoming increasingly important to me now that everything at Harold's was pumpkin spice flavored. I used to love getting those special lattes during the fall, but now that I'd been subjected to a PSL overdose at Kelley's hands, I firmly believed seasonal drinks were seasonal for a reason.

"What are you doing?" Merlin asked, hopping onto the counter and rubbing his face against the coffeemaker.

I pushed him to the side. "Don't do that. I hate it when you get your fur in my morning cuppa."

"But it's so warm and buzzy," he groaned.

"Speaking of warm and buzzy, I didn't like what I saw in the garden last night. I think it might be time to consider getting you and Luna fixed." My brain hadn't had the chance to wake up fully yet, but I still couldn't get that picture of them out of my head. It's like the disgusting scene was seared in my memory.

Merlin crept back up to the Keurig and rubbed his cheek against it again. This time he let out a contented purr as he asked, "Fixed? Why? We aren't broken. Well, I mean Luna's lost her magic, but other than that she's perfectly fine."

"It would be irresponsible to bring more kittens into the world, what with all the poor cats waiting in shelters." Also somehow I felt that my familiar duties would extend to playing nanny too, and my life was already complicated enough without having to be responsible for other living things—especially small and delicate living things.

"Wait. Are you saying—?" Merlin arched his back up and let out a terrible hiss. He even went so far as to take a swipe at me.

"You want to alter my privates? I thought such tales of human barbarism were but mere myths, made up to scare young witches at bedtime. But you... My own familiar? Please tell me you were joking!" He swooned and fell over onto his side, pumping his legs as if running in a dream. Apparently this is what a panic attack looked like on him.

Oops. I kept forgetting just how differently humans and cats viewed the world when it came to certain matters. Honestly, I should've known better on this one.

The coffee finished brewing, and I had to use a spoon to fish out the long, striped cat hair that had landed in my brew. I never should have initiated this conversation without a full cup of caffeine already buzzing through my system.

Unfortunately, since I'd started on this

topic, I now needed to finish it. "It's a minimally invasive surgery, especially for male cats."

Merlin popped back onto his feet, but his hackles were still raised. "If it's such an easy surgery, then why don't you have it?"

"It's not exactly the same for humans. Besides, I may want kids one day."

Merlin became Halloween cat again. Yup, I definitely wasn't winning any points with him this morning. "And you don't think Luna and I would like to pass our love down to the next generation? Besides, if you'll recall, I'm the last living descendant of the original Merlin. I can't let such an important magical bloodline die with me."

"But what about the shelter cats?" I whimpered pathetically.

"Look, heart to heart here. Luna has already lost her magic. Don't take motherhood away from her, too."

I raised an eyebrow, then took a careful sip from my mug. And still wound up with cat hair in my mouth. *Gross!*

The cat sighed. "Again your sense of morality confounds me. Still, if the shelter cats are so important to you, we'll find a way to help them. There's plenty of room in Nocturna. You get them here, and I can get them there."

"You promise?" I took another swig of my morning java.

"If that's what it takes to maintain peace in my home while also keeping my privates intact, then I agree." He came to the edge of the counter with his tail raised amicably, and I patted him softly on the head.

"Thank you. While we're talking openly about this, I do think you and Luna should wait to start your family."

"Why? We're already a bonded pair. Cats don't need a piece of paper telling us what we know to be true in our hearts."

"Be that as it may, we're kind of dealing with a lot right now. With the ghost. And we both know Dash will be back before too long. It just doesn't seem like the right time to bring a child—or, um, litter—into the world."

"Fair point. Now are you done with this strange heart to heart? Because I am very, very done."

I flushed. "Yes, sorry."

"I mean, you didn't even ask about the

ghost. After all the work we put in. You went straight to talking about my privates."

"You're right. I'm sorry. Now can we please stop talking about your privates?"

He shrugged. "If you don't want to talk about something, then don't start the conversation."

"Sorry, sorry, sorry. Now tell me about the ghost," I practically begged.

Merlin arched his back again, but this time in a stretch. He then jumped over to the table and waited for me to join him. "Well..." he began.

16

I hated when Merlin drew things out like this. "Well, what? Did we catch our ghost?" I demanded, and then realized something else strange about that morning. "Hey, where's Luna by the way?"

I almost never saw the cats apart from one another. Each morning when I woke up, they were together and basking in the glow of their new love.

Merlin sniffed at the air before responding to my questions. "Luna is out on a morning stroll. She said she needed some time to herself. From the smell of it, she's about two blocks out and making her return to us now."

Time to herself? Hmm. Did this mean trouble in paradise? The cats had already gone from lovers to bitter rivals and back to lovers again. I was beginning to think I had the Ross and Rachel of felines on my hands. They better not plan on taking a break any time soon, because I was so not prepared to deal with that!

I kept this all to myself, of course. Merlin and I had just been discussing family planning, and that hadn't gone over well. At all. I needed to resist the urge to play the role of therapist here. Those two were far more experienced in matters of the heart than I was, anyway.

When I didn't say anything in response to his news of Luna, Merlin continued on. This time telling me about the ghost. "It didn't come," he said with a bored yawn. "Luna and I waited all night, and that rotten ghost didn't even have the courtesy to drop in for a hello."

I gripped both hands around my coffee mug and sighed.

"That's a good thing, right? I mean, we don't actually want the ghost to be here."

"If it came here once, you can bet it will come again. By not returning last night, it's just drawing things out for everyone, and that irritates me." He flicked his tail to punctuate this remark.

"Maybe she knows we set a trap for her?" That would keep me away. Maybe it was stopping Virginia from returning as well.

"Maybe," he answered pensively. "I don't really know much about it. But I would assume she wouldn't know about the potion until she began to materialize, and by then, it would be too late." He had a point. There was so much we didn't know when it came to our baby ghost, and that made this whole thing so much harder.

The cat door flapped open noisily, and Luna came trotting inside.

"How was your walk, my love?" Merlin asked, then hopped down from the table to rub his face against hers. It was the scene with the coffeemaker all over again. Well, at least Luna was already covered in cat hair.

"It was nice to get some fresh air while I thought about why Virginia failed to visit us again last night," the white cat answered promptly.

Ah, so I'd been totally wrong about the

whole trouble in paradise thing. I was glad I hadn't pushed the issue. I really needed to butt out of my cats' relationship and let them handle things for themselves. Lesson learned.

"You need to stop blaming yourself," Merlin said softly.

They both jumped up on the table to reengage me in the discussion.

"Tell him, Gracie," Luna begged, her blue eyes fraught with remorse. "Virginia was my familiar. I chose her. I failed to see that she had been corrupted. It's all my fault."

I reached out to stroke her back. "Merlin's right. You really can't blame yourself. Bad things happen to good people—um, cats—sometimes. That's just the way of life."

"Well, then life sucks," she said with a sniff.

"Sometimes," I agreed. "But you have a lot to be grateful for. Why, just this morning Merlin—" I stopped short. I was doing it again, interfering in their relationship. "Told me how lucky he is to have you."

The Maine Coon winked at me, and Luna appeared to relax somewhat.

"What conclusions did you reach on your walk? Why didn't Virginia visit us?" I prompted when I grew tired of the extended silence. That was the thing about talking with cats. They were huge fans of the dramatic pause. They also had no sense of urgency, meaning simple conversations could draw out for hours if I didn't help to push them along.

"Maybe the ghost wasn't Virginia," Luna said. "Maybe it wasn't even here for us at all, but rather for the house."

"That's an interesting theory," I said slowly, even though I 100% disagreed with her assessment.

"If it's Virginia, we're prepared with our potion. If it's not, then we have nothing to fear," Merlin summarized.

"Yes, I suppose that's right," I said, taking another sip of my coffee. It was now dangerously close to room temperature, so I chugged it down fast and then rose to make a fresh cup.

"Anything else we should do about this now?" I asked while I sifted through my bucket of multi-flavored K-cups and selected a nice French roast.

"Now we wait," Merlin said in a bored drone. "Either the ghost will return and we can deal with it then, or it won't return at all, and we'll be in the clear."

Luna and I both nodded our agreement, but somehow I doubted it would be as simple as Merlin claimed.

And I think he knew that, too.

17

Several days passed with no more signs of our spectral visitor. As much as I'd doubted Luna's theory, I now had to admit it was fully possible that some ghost other than Virginia had dropped by. Just in case, though, I called my Grandma Grace to make sure she was alive and well. She didn't have much time to talk since life in her retirement community was full of exciting social events that were not to be missed, but she assured me she'd never felt better and would drive up to visit soon.

And so as the days ticked past, I focused on work and even managed to get some thesis research in. Drake and I chatted more at work than we had in the past, but I made every effort to keep all of our interactions platonic so that Kelley wouldn't be jealous and he wouldn't get the wrong idea about me.

He was an okay guy, but I had no time for close human relationships while I was settling into my role as familiar. And when eventually I did re-enter the dating pool, I needed someone with more direction and ambition than Drake. I could just picture the two of us drifting through life on handouts from my grandma and his parents while we both continued to work at the coffee shop until the day we died. That was not the life I wanted—nor the one I deserved.

Kelley at least had enough chutzpah for the both of them. They'd be a great couple, if Drake ever decided to return her feelings. Whatever the outcome, it would be interesting to watch their story unfold.

I, for one, was glad I had time to consider such matters. With each new day that passed, I worried less about the ghost. Each night I slept better. Each day I was able to focus on the people and cats in my life, try new makeup techniques, and just generally relax and enjoy myself.

It was divine.

I was right in the middle of a fantastic dream in which I won a lifetime supply of cosmetics from my favorite cruelty-free company, when—

Meeeeeeeh!

REOW! HISSS!

Meeeeeeh!

I bolted upright in bed as both cats continued to caterwaul in the hallway. This could only mean one thing. Our ghost had returned. And just when I was starting to believe our first visit had been a fluke.

I pulled on the robe that hung from the back of my door and stepped out into the hallway. Sure enough, both cats were going ballistic.

And I do mean ballistic.

Merlin had even begun kicking back his feet in that familiar chicken scratch maneuver, which meant—

"No! Stop! No lightning in the house!" I screamed, but my warning came too late.

A zipping bolt came crashing straight through the roof, illuminating the wayward spirit in the process. Suddenly a bright swatch of blue appeared right where my cats had been staring. Now I saw it, too.

Oh, Merlin. He'd meant to destroy the thing, but he'd only given it more power.

The house let out a giant whomp, and everything went silent—and even darker than before.

"Merlin, you fried the electricity," I shouted, unable to tear my eyes away from the transparent blue blob floating just a few feet away from me in the hallway.

And then it started to rain inside the house.

"Merlin!" I screamed.

"It wasn't me," he shouted back.

I raised my eyes and saw that—yes—the rain was coming through a newly made hole in the roof. That would not be cheap to repair. "You better be able to fix that with magic," I mumbled.

"You're worried about that when we now

have this?" Luna cried, motioning toward the ghost frantically.

The sudden motion startled the spirit, and it took off down the hall and moved on to rattling about the kitchen.

"Why wasn't it captured by your spell?" I demanded of the cats.

Meeeeeeeh!

REOW! HISSS!

Meeeeeeh!

Not the answer I was looking for. Clearly they weren't much help in this situation, given their desire to scream about the ghost rather than to capture it.

Come to think of it, I'd been shouting a lot, too. Ugh.

Never mind my initial reaction. Someone had to deal with this thing, and I guessed that someone might as well be me.

I marched into the kitchen and stumbled right into the table. Ouch!

The only light came from the ghost itself, thanks to Merlin's lightning-induced blackout. The pulsing blue blob didn't appear human, but what else could it be?

"Hey, Virginia," I called out, working hard

to hide the quiver in my voice. "Why are you here? What do you want?"

The ghost floated closer to me, and it took everything I had not to run out of the house screaming. I guess I couldn't hold the cats' reaction against them when I wished I could do the exact same thing.

The spirit continued to inch forward, slow as molasses. I could have run, but I stood transfixed, unable to pull my eyes away from the spectral sight.

Moments later, it completed its journey, stopping less than a foot in front of me.

And then it spoke in a terrible rasping echo that sent a shiver straight down my spine. "Who's Virginia?"

18

It was hard to tell given the strange echoing quality of its voice, but I was pretty sure our ghost was a boy.

"Who are you?" I murmured. I couldn't believe I was talking to a ghost. This topped all the strange things that had happened so far these past weeks. I'd reached a new peak of weirdness here and wasn't sure I liked it. Well, at least the spirit seemed gentle. That's definitely better than I'd have gotten were it actually Virginia.

"Gracie?" the ghost asked, moving so close to me that the glowing blue blob was but a hair's breadth from my face.

"Uh, ghost?" I responded stupidly.

"I never wanted to be a ghost," the strange creature moaned as its blue light undulated. "I don't know why I'm here, and I don't know why I came to you."

That was when I finally recognized something familiar in that eerie voice. This wasn't Virginia, but it was someone I'd known—someone I'd watched die not too long ago.

"Harold?" I asked in serious disbelief. "Is that you?"

"It's me," the spirit confirmed. Wow, I couldn't believe my former boss had returned from the spectral plane to pay me a visit. He'd hated me, and even more than that, he hated *paying me* anything—especially not what I was owed for all the hours I put in at his coffeeshop.

"No wonder the spell didn't work," I murmured to myself, thinking of the useless ceramic frog in the hallway. "It was made for Virginia. And you clearly aren't her."

"Who's Virginia?" Harold echoed.

"Don't worry about it," I shot back quickly. I really preferred not to tell him that Virginia was the one who had killed him in the first place. Instead, I swallowed hard and asked,

"Why are you here? Why did you come to see me, Harold?"

"I don't know," he answered as his blue light pulsed yet again. I wondered if the color he'd taken on was a coincidence or if it was something more of a mood ring. Would evil ghosts glow red? Magical ones green? Interesting to think about, but not what was important at the moment.

"Do you have unfinished business of some kind?" I asked after licking my dry lips.

"It's hard to remember much in this form," he said in that jarring echo of his. "But give me a moment, and I'll try."

While I waited for Harold to collect his thoughts, the two cats slowly moved out of the hallway and came to stand beside me in the kitchen.

"What does it want?" Merlin asked, swishing his tail so hard it thwapped me in the leg.

"A talking cat!" Harold exclaimed in fright and zipped back toward the sink.

"Yes, he's a talking cat, and you're a ghost. Which seems scarier to you?" I asked, tilting my head to the side in disbelief. "Besides, you just saw him talking in the hallway. You also watched him summon lightning, remember?"

"Oh, I think I do." The blobby blue Harold bobbed back over to us, coming dangerously close to crashing into Luna this time. "And this one threatened me!" the ghost cried when he recognized the white cat.

"I have a name. It's Luna," she hissed, arching her back at him.

"Eek! A talking cat!" Harold screamed and raced about the house.

Oh, boy. This was going to take a while.

I needed to take charge here, or we'd be at this all night. "Harold, you came for a reason. I know you're having a hard time remembering, so I'll ask some questions to see if that helps. Okay?"

He bobbed up and down, which I took to mean he agreed.

"Is this about how you died?" I ventured carefully.

"I was poisoned."

"Yes, that's good, Harold! Yes, you were poisoned." Oops, my voice sounded all high and babyish like it did when I talked to Merlin —before he started talking back, that is. When

I'd still assumed he was just a regular fuzzy wuzzy. Even though Harold seemed harmless, there was nothing fuzzy or wuzzy about the ghost before me.

"Well, you don't have to sound so happy about it," he booed.

"Oh, trust me. I'm not happy about it."

Sigh. I might as well tell him the truth and get it off my chest. He'd forget it in a few seconds any way. "I'm sorry, too. You were murdered because someone wanted to hurt me."

"But she avenged you," Merlin added, hopping up onto the table to get closer to the talking blue orb. "She risked her own life to punish those who hurt you."

"So my killer is now dead?" Harold wanted to know.

I shrugged for lack of a better response. "Um, yes and no. The mastermind is still on the loose, but the one who pulled the trigger is definitely dead."

"No, I wasn't shot. I was poisoned," he insisted in another wailing echo.

"Right." No tangents, no metaphors. Straight simple language. "Does your visit have anything to do with your daughter? Kelley?"

"My daughter," the ghost mumbled and then flashed bright cerulean and shouted, "Kelley! Yes, I wanted to thank you for helping her."

I smiled. Harold would have been a good dad if he'd been given more of a chance. "Of course I helped her, she's my friend."

"But you gave her your one wish. You didn't have to do that."

My jaw would have hit the floor if it could reach. "You couldn't remember that cats can talk, but somehow you both knew and remembered that my cat brewed a potion which I then gave to Kelley so her biggest dream could come true?"

The blue blob tilted to the side. "Memory is strange as a ghost. It comes and goes."

"Well, you're welcome for helping Kelley. She wants to do your legacy proud. You have a very good daughter there. It's too bad you didn't get much of a chance to know her."

Harold's hue turned dark like midnight. "It is too bad."

"Tomorrow is the grand re-opening of the

coffeehouse. She kept the name," I informed him. "To honor you."

He brightened once more. "Would you please tell her I'm proud of her?"

Well, this was sweet and all, but I really needed to get some sleep since I was scheduled to work a double shift tomorrow. "I'll see what I can do. Thank you for the visit, Harold. Was that all?"

"Wait!" The ghost raced around the kitchen before returning to face me. "I have a warning to deliver from the other side."

"That might have been a good thing to start with," Merlin said snippily.

I shushed him, then softened my voice to speak to Harold. "What is the message?"

His voice grew deep and clear, changed. "Seeds that have been sown will soon bear dangerous fruit."

I gasped. "Harold? What does that mean?"

He spun slowly as if surveying the room. "What does what mean?"

"The message you just gave me," I pressed. Please remember, please rememb—

"I don't remember," he said and then flashed out of view.

19

The next morning I woke up with a killer headache. Not only had the whole fiasco in the kitchen taken an unpredictably long time, but when it was over I lay awake for close to an hour pondering the meaning of Harold's ghostly warning.

Seeds that have been sown will soon bear dangerous fruit.

What did that mean?

For all I knew, Harold heard it in some movie before he died and now summoned it back up, confusing it for a real memory. It certainly sounded like some weird prophecy that had come straight out of an epic fantasy film.

The more I thought about it, the more confused I became. I guessed I'd just have to wait and see what happened next, as much as I hated not being able to prepare.

It would be a busy day.

The coffeehouse's grand re-opening had arrived. I had to give her credit, Kelley had made especially fast progress in retooling the menu and retraining the staff. Now the moment of her public debut as owner of Harold's House of Coffee had arrived.

She'd need all hands on deck because today was going to be non-stop busy. The magic I'd secretly given to her guaranteed it would be so.

At my urging, Kelley had scheduled the full staff to work a double shift for the day, including me.

When I arrived at Harold's, I found her wearing a white '50s inspired party dress with little pumpkins and horns of plenty patterned all over it. She ran over to me with a huge grin on her face. "Gracie, hello! Are you ready for our big day?"

"Your big day," I reminded her with a grin. "And yes, I'm definitely ready." No need to let her know I'd lost several good hours of sleep last night, thanks to the paranormal soap opera my life had become.

She nodded, and a pair of jack-o-lantern earrings bobbed along with her. "Good news, the new uniform shirts arrived last night. Grab one from the office and get changed."

Oh, no. Harold had allowed us to wear whatever we wanted because he was too cheap to invest in uniforms, but Kelley had gone all out by commissioning a series of custom T-shirt designs that would change each month.

I sifted through the box until I found a large, then pulled it on over my other shirt. On the front, my new uniform said "#PSLISBAE," which was the new hashtag Kelley was trying to get started on social media. The back read, "Ask me about my favorite pumpkin spice!"

Lord help us all.

When I came back out of the office, I found Kelley standing near the creamer station and staring up at the wall. As I drew closer, I discovered she was studying a framed picture that hadn't been there when last I worked two days ago.

The photo was the same one that had been

on display by the casket for Harold's funeral. It was a close-up of his face, complete with chubby cheeks, narrow eyes, and receding hairline. Kelley should thank her lucky stars that she'd inherited her good looks from her mother.

"Do you think he'd be proud of me?" she whispered when I reached her side.

"I know he would be," I said giving her shoulder a supportive squeeze.

Kelley turned toward me but didn't meet my eye. "Really?" she mumbled. "You don't think I'm overdoing it with the pumpkin spice?"

"People are going to love it. Just you wait."

Now she looked at me. Her eyes held all her dreams and secret fears. This was so much more than a grand opening to her. It was an opportunity to bond with the father she'd only just begun to know. "What makes you so sure?" she asked.

"I just know," I assured her, and then, "Hey, should we take a couple quick shots of pumpkin roast espresso to help get us pumped?"

"That's a great idea," she gushed, stepping

past me and rushing toward the industrial sized espresso maker. "Everyone gather around!" she called as she worked the machine.

The three new hires had already arrived. I'd been so focused on my many magical problems this past week that I hadn't really made any efforts to get to know them outside of Kelley's team-building activities. Now that I knew our ghostly visitor had been Harold of all people, maybe I could start to relax even more. To let other people in.

Drake flew through the door just as Kelley was pouring the last shot into a little paper cup. "Sorry I'm late!"

"Actually you're five minutes early," Kelley said as she handed him a shot.

Drake jerked his head toward the door. "Should I go back out and come in a little later?"

"Oh, stop." Kelley hit his chest playfully, and I watched as standoffish, sarcastic Drake blushed. He actually blushed! Perhaps there was hope for these two, after all.

"A toast!" I said, raising my own paper cup in the air.

"To Harold's. Long may his legacy live!" Kelley cheered.

"To Kelley. Long may she overlook my tardiness!" Drake countered.

"To all things pumpkin spice," I added.

The newbies shouted a combination of "Cheers!" and "Hear, hear!"

And then we all took down our shots of espresso.

"Ah, hot, hot, hot!" I cried.

"That went straight up my sinuses," Drake whined.

The others just laughed and laughed.

Yup, we were ready to slay.

20

I dragged myself home at the end of my double shift, reeking of cinnamon, nutmeg, and ginger. As much as my feet ached and my back twinged, I couldn't be happier. Kelley had truly risen to the occasion, and I loved seeing the way her face lit up as she basked in the success of a job well done.

I was happy, but now very ready to unwind.

Thank goodness the power outage last night had been the result of a sudden electrical overload and not permanent wire damage. A quick trip to my house's fuse box had restored power. The hole in the roof, on the other hand, would be much more difficult to fix.

I tried not to worry about it as I popped a

TV dinner in the microwave, then settled on the couch and scrolled through Netflix. After my hard day of work, I deserved to indulge in the sleaziest, most over-the-top reality series I could find. I settled on one of their original series that asked people to get engaged before ever meeting face-to-face. This would be trashy television gold.

And, yeah, it was interesting right away. I could hardly tear my eyes from the screen when the microwave dinged, alerting me that my slimmed down version of mac and cheese was ready for consumption.

So transfixed I was by the ridiculousness playing out on screen that I accidentally stumbled over one of the cats on my way to the kitchen.

Luna mewled and ran to my bedroom for cover.

"How dare you!" Merlin boomed, marching straight up to me from wherever he'd been.

"I'm sorry, Luna! It was an accident!" I called after the retreating feline.

Then I turned toward Merlin. "Don't lecture me when you put a hole in our roof just last night! I called a fix-it company for a rough quote while I was on break, and they want more than I make in a month! So I hope you've learned your lesson about summoning the elements inside our house."

"Don't start a family. Don't summon lighting. You have so many rules!" the giant fluff of a cat spat.

I scoffed at him. "They're very reasonable rules."

"I think you're forgetting who's in charge here. I'm the witch."

"And I'm the homeowner," I exploded. I seriously didn't have one drop of energy left to deal with his nonsense today. "I'm also the one who pays all the bills. And I've just had a very long, tiring day at work, so don't push me!"

"You're lucky you're not a cat, or I'd challenge you to a duel right here and right now." He stamped his little kitty foot in rage, but it didn't scare me either.

"Merlin! Gracie!" Luna cried. "Enough!"

We both looked to her and grimaced.

"It was an accident, and I'm fine." As she approached I noticed something different about the way she moved. Oh, I really hoped I hadn't hurt her too badly with my careless mistake. "But you two have both been way too tense lately. Remember, we are all on the same side."

Merlin moaned. "But she—"

"But nothing. We're all dealing with a lot right now, and the last thing we need is to start turning on each other. You're both stressed, and I understand. I think you need a bit of space to cool off from each other."

"I'm sorry, Luna. You're right. I'm just really stressed about the ghost and the warning I can't make heads or tails of, and the hole in the roof, and—"

"I know you are, dear. I would fix the hole for you if I could, and I would have been able to, if I still had my magic. Never matter, Merlin will travel to Nocturna at the first available moment and find a garden witch who can assist with the repairs."

"But Tom Cat!" Merlin argued. "If he sees me, he'll challenge me again. I could die, Luna. Die!"

"Then you'll just have to make sure he doesn't see you," she coaxed. "Now I want the two of you to make up this instant."

"I'm sorry, Merlin," I said, casting my eyes

to the floor. Luna was good at the whole disappointed parent thing. She'd make a great mother one day when she and Merlin were officially ready to start their family.

Luna walked over to Merlin and nudged him with her paw. "Now you."

"Sorry, Gracie," he muttered while also rolling his eyes.

Luna nodded, missing that last gesture. "Now, Gracie, why don't you get back to your show? Merlin, let's go on a date. It may be our last chance before the children are born."

"What?" I exploded.

"Run, my love, run!" Merlin cried as they both launched themselves at the cat door.

Well, that was one more huge thing to worry about. Perhaps I should stop assuming that life would settle down and get back to normal. Chaos was the new normal. And soon kittens!

For today, however, I let the melodramatic reality show soothe my anxieties somewhat as I chowed down on my soggy cheese noodles.

And I didn't even make it to the end of the first episode before I drifted off on the couch.

21

I awoke sometime later, confused at first as to where I was. Then I spotted the message from Netflix on my TV screen: *Are you still watching?*

I switched off the television with its remote, then sat up and stretched my arms overhead. I needed to move myself into bed, but I was still so, so sleepy.

Just as I was about to force myself to stand, I heard a series of clicks and scratches coming from across the living room. *What the heck?*

I tiptoed over to take a look and saw the silhouette of a cat in the window. My cat.

"Merlin, what are you doing out there?" I cried, racing to open the window.

But before I could make it across the room, a bright green light burst forth from the wall and blocked my path.

"Harold?" I squeaked, even though there was no mistaking the figure before me.

"So we meet again," a ghostly Virginia drawled. Unlike Harold, she was much more than an amorphous glowing orb. Her face was fully formed in a perfect replica of how she had looked in life—except now she was green and semi-transparent. She was also missing most of her body. In fact, her figure ended slightly below the armpits, giving her a bust-like appearance.

Virginia charged at me and gnashed her teeth.

I dodged out of the way just in time. "Get out of here, and leave us alone," I shouted, running for the hallway.

Virginia followed, cackling as if she were a witch and not a ghost. Maybe she was a witch now, too. She was certainly glowing green with magic, which put me at a double disadvantage. I couldn't wield any power of my own, and I had zero idea how to kill a ghost. *Wonderful.*

I groped about in the corner of the hallway

until I found the ceramic frog with the potion pooled within its open maw. As soon as I got a firm grip on it, I spun and thrust it toward my assailant.

"Take that!" I shouted, proud of my quick thinking despite the fog of fatigue that enveloped me.

"What are you doing with my frog?" Virginia asked with a dry laugh. "And why are you waving it at me like a weapon?"

I braced myself with feet shoulder width apart. "I hereby bind you, ghost!"

"Silence." Virginia's bellow echoed, reverberating through the entire house.

I pushed the frog at her again, but it flew from my hands and crashed into the wall. When I tried to speak, I found my mouth was sealed shut.

"That's better," Virginia said with an approving nod. "Now enough with the theatrics. I'm here to kill you. Nothing more, nothing less. You'll pay for what you and your witch did. I have more magic in death than I ever had in life, and now I will use it to avenge my untimely death. So, any last words?"

She rotated her head on her stump of a torso and released her magical hold on me.

I gasped, then shouted at her the second I was able to move my mouth. "Where are my cats?"

Her green dulled with apparent disappointment. "Well, that's a waste of words. If you must know, I've magically sealed this house. They can't get in, and you can't get out. You're entirely at my mercy. First I'll take care of you, and then I'll finish them off as well. It's almost too easy."

"You don't have magic. H-h-how is this possible?" I sputtered. If I could keep her talking, I could keep me breathing.

Virginia had such a large ego she not only wanted to murder me, but she also wanted me to bask in her brilliance before she did it. The quintessential villain divulging her master plan instead of actually implementing it.

"Oh, anything is possible if you have the right friends. Luna was an amateur, a fool! But my new master appreciates what I am, what I can do." She was so textbook bad guy, I almost felt sorry for her. Unfortunately, I felt much sorrier for me in this moment, though. Virginia had no morals that I had seen, and she wouldn't hesitate to deliver on her promise of my demise.

Even though I was still shaking in my boots, I forced myself to roll my eyes. "Dash, you mean? You're still working for that witch after the last time literally got you killed?"

"I know what you're doing, and I'm not stupid enough to fall for it," a glowing, green Virginia hissed.

"Funny choice of words. Fall for it? Isn't that how you died the first time? Maybe it's how you'll die this time, too?" I would have crossed my arms over my chest, but I needed to have them ready in case Virginia flew at me again.

"I am immortal in my new form!" she boomed triumphantly. "The only one dying tonight will be you. And your little kitty friends." She hurled herself at me with her ghostly mouth wide open and clamped down on my shoulder.

Ouch, ouch, ouch. It hurt so bad! Much more than any bite should have stung. Somehow I knew she had infected me with magic.

But what kind?

And what would it do?

I swooned on my feet. No, I couldn't let her win.

Especially not so easily.

But then I swooned again.

"What did you do to me?" I croaked.

22

"I created a drain. Soon the magic within you will begin flowing to me," Virginia revealed, circling me with glee. "And once I have enough of it, I will use it to end you. How's that for poetic justice?"

Virginia sure was full of herself. But even I had to admit that her plan was a good one. Killing me with my own well of magic.

Just wow.

I hadn't even made it a full month as a familiar, and already my ties to the magical world had led to my imminent death.

Sorry, but no.

I was not going down without a fight.

My cats couldn't get inside to help me, but I

could still hear them at the window. I could still talk to them, let them guide me in this battle. I hurled myself down the hall, passing straight through the enemy ghost, and raced to the living room window.

Merlin sat waiting as I unlatched the window and pried it open. "Gracie, behind you!" he shouted.

I dodged to the side to avoid another painful bite from my spectral opponent.

Virginia passed through the window, screamed in rage, and then hurled herself back the other way.

"She used most of her magic to create her barrier spell," Luna called from out of sight. "It's why half her body's missing. Even with the drain she placed on you, she is regenerating very slowly."

Yes, Luna was right! By silencing me, she'd lost her stumpy little arms. Her figure now ended at the collarbone. If she cast another big spell, she might blink herself out of existence.

The ghost drove at me again, and I leapt out of the way. Were all these physical attacks meant to distract me while she recharged her magic? And what was the worst she could do to me without magic? Bite me again? That would hurt, but I already knew I could survive it.

Well, two could play at her little game of wait and see.

I ran to the closet and grabbed my broom.

Virginia laughed at me, mocking my choice of weapon. But then I slammed it into her face, grody bristles first, and sent her flying backward.

"You'll pay for that!" she promised, her green transforming into a blazing emerald as she spat curses at me. "Freeze!"

My feet fused to the floor. I could still move my upper body, but the lower part was now stuck like a fly in honey.

As soon as she muttered this magical command, the rest of her ghostly shoulders disappeared from view. Now she was just a bobbing head and a neck.

"You can't kill me without killing yourself," I said as if this were fact and not just my current theory. She'd told me she was now immortal as a ghost, but that didn't mean she could stay on our earthly plane for long.

"I'm already dead, thanks to you!" she

bandied back. As her frustration grew, her words came out faster, more slurred together.

"Gracie!" Merlin shouted from the window. I glanced through Virginia and saw both he and Luna sitting on the sill now.

"We can bind her, but I'll need ingredients from my garden," the she-cat yelled.

"No, the frog didn't work." If it had, this whole thing would have stopped almost as soon as it started. If only.

Luna didn't give up, however. "It was too old and lost its potency, but a new batch will work."

"I can't leave."

"Try the door," Merlin shouted. Thank you, captain obvious.

"I can't. I'm stuck." I motioned toward my legs and let out a groan.

This whole time Virginia was shouting insults at us but not actually casting any more spells. It seemed I was right about her not having the requisite power to finish the deed she'd come to commit. She probably hadn't realized how much the barrier spell would take out of her. It's not like she was a real witch, anyway. She'd never had magic in life and was inexperienced with it in death.

I scanned the room, all the while searching for some kind of solution that would unstick me from the floor. I spotted my phone lying on the coffee table a good six feet away. I couldn't reach out and grab it, but I did have a broom in my hands. If I could distract Virginia long enough to get ahold of it, I could send an SOS text to Drake.

Luckily he'd insisted on programming my number into his phone after our failed date. He'd also offered to help with my ghost, should I need it. And I definitely needed it right now.

"Hey, loser!" I shouted loud enough for Virginia to hear me over her deranged ranting. "Think fast!"

23

I pretended to cast a spell. Yes, I couldn't use the magic within me, and, yes, Virginia knew that. But thankfully my ruse still worked.

I raised the hand that wasn't holding my broom and made an elaborate twisty gesture. "Merlin, lightning!" I cried.

Sure enough, Virginia spun around just in time to see Merlin summon a bolt of lightning right outside the window. His magic couldn't cross the barrier she'd erected, but the ghostess couldn't help but watch transfixed as Merlin's attempt to come to my aid "failed."

Quick as a shot, I swept my broom to the side, then pulled it back to me like an oar. This sent my phone skittering across the floor and straight toward me. Thank goodness I'd invested in a good phone case, or this plan would not have worked.

I stooped down still rooted to the spot and grasped the phone in my hands. With a quick swipe to unlock it, I opened my contacts and typed a quick message, both of my thumbs flying impossibly fast over the screen.

Drake, SOS!

Come help me!

I sent each text separately, not knowing when Virginia would manage to wrest the phone from my hands and silence my cries for help.

Ghost is— Virginia reeled back around and tore the phone from my hands with her magic before I could finish. It flew and smashed against the wall, much the same as the frog had. So much for that heavy-duty case.

RIP, my iPhone.

Drake would come. I knew he would. What he'd be able to do to help, now there was a question I hadn't quite thought out.

I studied Virginia to see if any more of her had faded from view, thanks to her most recent use of magic, but it seemed she had lost no ground. Which meant the drain she'd placed on me was beginning to work.

No, no, no. What else could I do to stall her?

"Merlin, I'm scared!" I shouted, making Virginia positively glow with *schadenfreude*.

"I won't leave you," he promised from his spot at the window. "Even through the barrier spell, my presence is keeping you strong. And yours is also protecting me."

"But the drain..." My words fell away as if my energy was also being sucked from me along with the magic.

Merlin stood and pressed his paws against the barrier, giving me a full view of his furry tummy. "It's my magic you carry. A small part of it is going to Virginia, but most of it is able to escape to the barrier and come back to me. I can't leave or the magic will have no place else to go."

"Stop helping her!" Virginia raged, but she was also unable to cast through the barrier. To land an attack on Merlin, she'd need to go outside. And we all knew he was a much more powerful magic user than she was, especially with my additional energy flowing into him now.

"You're stuck until you've generated enough magic to enact whatever death spell you have planned." Merlin addressed the ghost directly, his voice cold and haughty.

To me, he said, "Ignore her. She can't hurt you yet."

"Oh, yes, I can!" Virginia screamed and then lunged and bit me again. She came at me so fast, I hadn't been ready with my broom. Darn it!

This new wound throbbed with pain, but I could survive it. She couldn't bite me to death, and right now my primary objective was to not die. Honestly, it was kind of my only objective.

"Memorize this list of ingredients," Luna called to me from beside Merlin. "When your boyfriend gets here, send him straight to my garden. If he brings back what we need, Merlin and I can make a new binding potion."

"But he'll see you practicing magic and hear you talking!" I objected. Merlin had drilled it into my head from the start that I could not reveal magic to non-magical people. What was the point of surviving my ghostly encounter only to wind up in a dingy prison for the rest of my life?

Luna's voice came to me strong and confident. "We have not revealed ourselves to him, so he will only hear meows. And his eyes will invent other scenarios to explain away our actions. Everything will be fine. Just be careful. Now memorize this list. Hawthorn, celandine…"

Luna shouted out at least ten ingredients, and we went over them again and again until she was sure I had them all right.

Virginia continued to spit and howl, but at worst she only made us repeat ourselves a few times to be heard over the din.

Why did it feel like my epic magical encounters always dragged out? Life-or-death confrontations in movies always happened so fast. There was no waiting for a ghost's magic to recharge or biding time until the correct potion could be brewed.

Real magic was both more exciting and much more boring than the magic in the movies. At least the movies couldn't kill me.

Virginia, on the other hand…

She swept toward me again, and I hit her

away with the broom. I was getting kind of good at this. She rounded back to attack again, but a pair of bright white lights burst through the window, interrupting her efforts.

Drake had arrived.

24

*E*verything seemed to stop as Virginia and I waited mid-battle for Drake to turn off his engine, exit the car, and come inside.

He pounded on the front door. "Gracie! Is everything okay? Let me in!"

The barrier spell! Would he even be able to enter? And if he did, would he be able to get out again?

"Drake," I cried out, my voice hoarse from all the screaming I'd been doing that night. "Don't come in!"

"What's going on?" he demanded, rattling the doorknob, but it remained shut tight.

"Don't come in!" I begged, hoping he wouldn't waste time arguing. I needed him to act and act fast. "Please, I need your help. I need you to go to a garden and get me a list of ingredients."

Drake pounded on the door with all he had. "What? Gracie, why? What's going on? Is the ghost back? Are you okay?"

"It's here, and it's very angry. I need to bind it before—"

"I'm not an it! Show some respect, you weak mortal!" Virginia hissed and swooped around the room.

"Whoa," Drake cried, and his pounding stopped. "Was that the ghost? You're right, it does sound angry!"

"It, it, it! I am not an it! And you, foolish boy, have just been added to my hit list," Virginia was in fine form, glowing the brightest I'd seen yet. Pride was an important sticking point for her. Hmm, maybe if Drake came in he could talk her to death by getting her to use her magic so much she dematerialized, but I couldn't risk his safety. And I also much preferred ridding myself of her permanently. It was Luna's potion or bust. I just needed to convince Drake to leave and get what she needed.

"Drake, it's okay. Don't listen to her," I called, hoping that Virginia's threats hadn't caused him to lose courage. "Just go to the garden. Bring back what we need. It's the only way. Do you have your phone? Take down this list."

A brief moment of silence, and then, "I'm ready."

I recited the ingredients to Luna's nodding approval and also gave Drake the address. "Now hurry please! I'm counting on you!"

I listened as Drake's feet slapped the pavement in retreat, then his engine roared to life and he sped away.

"What now?" I asked the cats who were both still watching from the windowsill.

"We wait and hope that he brings us the correct ingredients. And swiftly," Luna answered.

"Drake knows a little bit about a lot of things," I said, recalling the conversation I'd had first with him and then with Kelley. "Gardening is one of them. Besides, he can always look up the ingredients on his phone and make sure he's picking the right ones. He won't mess this up."

For some reason, I believed this with every fiber of my being. Drake would not let me down. In fact, he would save me. Everything would be okay.

I just had to be patient.

"I'm growing stronger by the minute," Virginia reminded me in a serpentine whisper. And she was right. She'd regained the form she had when I first saw her—a full bust that filled out to just a little below her armpits. "I will kill you, Gracie, and I will make your boyfriend watch. Then I'll rebuild my power and kill him, too. Next will be Luna. I'm saving my former master for last. Before the night is through, you will all be dead."

"No one is dying today, you old goose," Merlin heckled her through the barrier. "Especially not my familiar and not my unborn children!"

Virginia gasped and spun toward the window. "What did you say?"

"We have the power of love on our side. Your hate will never win," I yelled, because that seemed like the type of thing a good guy would say in a showdown like this.

"It seems I left you at the right time, Luna," Virginia said coldly. "At least as a witch, you had some power. But you gave that all up, didn't you? And for what? To play house with some walking hairball and to bear his brats?"

"I owe you nothing, Virginia," Luna ground out, a growl underlying the words. "And you can never understand that power comes in many forms. My children will grow to be strong and kind and to help rid the world of monsters like you."

"They will die or live cursed lives. That I can guarantee." As the ghost shared this eerie promise, I knew better than to doubt her words.

As much as I'd thought this wasn't the right time for my cats to start a family, I would fight with everything I had to protect Luna's litter. Virginia had meant to scare us, but she'd only given me more motivation.

I would defeat her once and for all.

Those kittens would never know how close they'd come to ending before they'd ever had a chance to begin.

Auntie Gracie was on the case.

And she would not let them down.

25

By the time Drake returned, Virginia's ghostly body had materialized down to her navel.

And those twenty-odd minutes of waiting, trapped in place, while she ranted and raved and told us all how awful we were, proved to be among the most excruciating of my life. A few times she charged at me, but I was able to deftly knock her away with my broomstick.

Honestly, I think we were both relieved when Drake's car pulled into my driveway for the second time that night. This time, however, two sets of footsteps approached my door instead of just one.

"Drake?" I called out warily. *Please let it be him. Please let it be him.*

"It's me," he called through the door.

"And me," a second voice chimed.

"Kelley?" I croaked. Why on earth would he have knowingly brought her into a dangerous situation? Now that my friends were at risk, too, I felt the pressure mount. Me, Luna, Merlin, the kittens, Drake, Kelley—I had to save us all and fast. Virginia was reforming more and more quickly. Soon she'd be able to cast whatever she had planned for me, and then she'd take us all out one by one.

"I ran into her at that house," Drake shouted to explain Kelley's presence. "How come you didn't tell me it was hers? Anyway, she wanted to help, so I brought her back with me. Now will you please let us in?"

"No, don't come in!" I shouted, but it was too late.

Virginia used a small bit of her accumulated magic to throw the door open and pull both Kelley and Drake inside.

"Gracie, what's going on?" Kelley trembled as she caught sight of Virginia's imposing presence.

"Whoa," Drake said on the wings of an exhale. "Why is she green?"

"She has magic. She trapped me inside, and now I fear she's trapped you as w-well," I sputtered. I was determined to win, but also terrified I wouldn't be able to. We needed to mix the potion in the cauldron and either lure Virginia outside or bring the mix inside to bind her. But how, if no one could move through the barrier without her consent?

Virginia must have realized this as well, because she chose that exact moment to let out a textbook perfect evil laugh. "And now you've brought me one more. I shall kill her, too."

Kelley choked out a sob, which only made Virginia laugh harder. Oh, she would pay for that!

Drake took Kelley in his arms and made soft shushing noises. "I'll protect you," he promised, then glanced up toward me. "Both of you."

"She's erected a barrier around the house. Nobody can go out or come in unless she allows it. And I can't move from this spot," I explained, gesturing toward my useless legs.

"Yeah, no. I'm not letting some ninja turtle

looking banshee tell me what I can and can't do," Drake declared. He guided Kelley into my waiting arms and then marched back toward the front door.

No, no, no. For all I knew the barrier was electrified. Sure, it hadn't hurt Merlin when he touched it, but Drake wasn't magical. Could he withstand the sudden shock of making contact?

"Drake, stop!" I yelled. "She—"

But then he stepped outside. Turning to me, he pushed his hair back with a flip and flashed us all a debonair grin. "You were saying?"

"How is this possible?" Virginia screamed and spun around the house.

At the same time, Kelley launched herself from my arms and went flying toward the door. When she reached the threshold, though, she slammed into it with a *thwack* and fell backward with a heavy thud. "I don't understand," she sobbed. "Why can he leave, but I can't?"

Drake reached through the doorway and offered her his hand, but hard as he tried, he couldn't pull her through. When he let her go,

Kelley pushed herself against the wall and curled into a whimpering ball.

"How did you do that?" I demanded of him. And would I be able to do it, too, once I was able to move from this exact spot on the floor?

Drake shrugged. "I don't know. Sometimes I can just do stuff others can't. Or sometimes I just know things, like how I knew where you lived without you telling me."

"You followed me," I said, preferring the explanation that made more sense. Even if it was creepy and stalkerish.

He shook his head. "Nope, I just pulled it from of my memory. Weird thing is I don't remember making the memory in the first place, but there it was, ready to be of service."

"Enough of this," Virginia seethed. "Let me recharge in peace."

"Why would we do anything for you?" I snapped. "You're just going to kill us."

"And, oh, how I am looking forward to that." She flashed bright as her ghostly hips now started to materialize. We were running out of time.

"Drake, take the ingredients you got from the garden to the birdbath in the front yard, mix everything together, and then put it in some kind of container and bring it back inside."

"How much of each thing? I mean, if I'm making a recipe, surely there are certain measurements required to get it right?"

He had a point. But how could he be so nonchalant about this all? I'd already known all about magic, and yet I was terrified. Kelley lay curled in the fetal position, but Drake was fine with talking casually about everything?

"I... I don't know," I mumbled.

But then Luna appeared outside the open door and promptly introduced herself to Drake. "Hi, I'm a cat. I used to be a witch, but I'm not anymore. Still, I can help you save Gracie if you'll let me guide you in making this potion."

Drake stared at her with wide eyes.

Kelley's sobbing intensified.

I waited, afraid to look away. Afraid of what would happen next.

Drake let out a long, stuttering sigh. "Yeah, okay, cat lady. Let's go do the thing."

26

It was agony not being able to watch Luna and Drake prepare the potion. Merlin did move to the open doorway to offer an update, but Virginia quickly slammed the door in his face. He then moved back to the window so that the magic flowing out of me would have an easier time reaching him.

"Gracie, do you have a pitcher or something?" Drake called, charging back through the front door so easily Virginia shook and flashed with rage.

"Never mind. Found one," he called out a moment later. As he passed by me, I realized he'd taken the same pitcher I'd used as a vase for the flower he gifted me. I wondered if he noticed.

He stopped before reaching the door, then turned to address me again. "Oh, the cat lady said I need a piece of some frog to finish the potion. Know where I can get that?"

That's right. We still needed something that had belonged to Virginia. Even though her little garden creature had shattered, those shards could still be of use. That was a relief.

"Hallway," I directed Drake, jerking my head to the side, and he took off to retrieve the needed ingredient.

He held up a shiny piece of ceramic as he took his return trip through the living room. "Got it."

Virginia shrieked and threw herself at him.

I tried to push her away with my broom, but she and Drake were both beyond my reach. "Look out!" I cried helplessly.

Drake glanced up just as Virginia crashed into him... Or rather, through him.

"What are you?" she cried in a quavering voice.

"What are you?" he shot back, then seeing

that he was unaffected by her advance, carried on toward the door.

He disappeared outside and returned a couple moments later carrying the pitcher now filled with murky green potion. "The cat lady said to give this to you," he said, placing the vessel in my hands.

"But what do I do with it?" I offered Drake my broom in exchange.

He didn't have time to answer before Virginia came flying at us.

He tried to bat her away, but the broom in his hands passed straight through her.

The angry spirit tackled me, and I would have fallen flat on my butt if not for the fact she'd frozen me in place earlier during this encounter.

I remained standing tall, the pitcher clutched firmly within my hands.

Virginia, on the other hand...

"What is happening?" she cried as all the color drained from her form and swirled into the pitcher.

I watched in awe as my vessel filled with pure light, magic.

When I looked back up at Virginia, she was

drab and gray. She'd also regained her full body all the way to the tips of her ghostly toes.

"You stole my magic. Give it back!" she hissed and grabbed for the pitcher, but her hand passed straight through. She tried again, only to receive the same result.

"Where'd she go?" Drake asked, still holding the useless broom like a baseball bat.

I pointed straight ahead. "She's right here. Can't you see her?"

"No, Gracie. She's definitely gone." He let out a dry laugh as if he thought I was trying to trick him.

Merlin's voice floated to me through the open window. "We couldn't dispatch her fully because her unfinished business is killing you, Gracie. Until that's fulfilled, she will be trapped in our realm."

"Then how do we get rid of her?" I asked, craning my neck to search for him, but he was gone from the window.

"I will kill you!" Virginia growled and dove at me, but remained invisible to the others.

"The potion we brewed relieved her of her magic and bound her to this house," Luna announced after she and Merlin ran inside through the cat flap. It seemed that Virginia's barrier spell had fallen when she lost her magic.

"So she's stuck here? With us?" I screeched. Our house was full enough as it was, especially with kittens on the way. The last thing we needed was another roommate, especially one whose greatest desire was to kill us all.

"Yes, but she can't harm us. Or anyone else." Luna nodded slowly. I guessed she didn't like this arrangement any better than I did.

"Die, brat, die!" Virginia swooped at me once more, but the harder she worked to get my attention, the more her voice and image faded.

"Also you're not stuck. You can move again," Merlin informed me, nudging my foot with his paw. "So stop standing there, and move."

I jerked my foot upward, expecting the simple movement to be extraordinarily difficult. But this only resulted in my losing my balance and stumbling into Drake.

He caught me and helped me stand up tall. "Careful there, compadre."

"That's the second time you've called me that," I told him with a curious glance. "Why?"

"It's just a colorful way of reminding myself I live in the friend zone," he said with a wink. "And it's especially important now that I know you're this awesome witch who fights evil spirits on the regular."

Ugh. That was right. Drake pretty much knew all my secrets now. Sure, he didn't know about my Arthurian ancestry or the fact I was a familiar rather than a witch, but he still knew way too much.

I hoped the cats had a plan for dealing with that, and also that I wouldn't be heading to a wretched magical prison for sharing too much with a mortal.

I may have had a hard time with the ghost, but I'd still beaten her. I doubted I would have such an easy experience with hardened magical criminals while trapped inside an inescapable box.

27

"Hello? Is it safe to come out now?" a haunting voice echoed through the walls.

"Let me go!" Virginia cried, but her words were hardly more than a whisper now. At least that would make it easier to ignore her, if we would truly be living together for—what?—the rest of my life now, I guessed. Besides, Drake and Kelley clearly couldn't see or hear her anymore. Not even a little bit. That, at least, was a relief.

"Is that you, Harold?" I called out.

A blue hand reached through the living room wall and offered me a thumbs up. Nice to see he was coming into his full form now.

Kelley glanced toward me with glistening eyes. "M-my d-dad?" she sputtered. "Is he really here?"

"C'mon out, Harold!" I called with a smile. And it felt so good to feel my cheeks rise in happiness that I actually laughed aloud.

Harold phased into the living room. He was still mostly a blob, but he did have hands and a face, which was something.

Kelley slowly pushed herself to her feet but hung back from our new arrival.

"It's okay," I assured her with another smile. "He's not like the other one. C'mon."

When I motioned to her, she came over to stand beside me. "Dad?" she asked, unsure that a ghost could be trusted, even if it was one she'd known in life.

"Kelley," Harold responded in that melodic echo of his.

She kept her wide eyes directed at Harold, but spoke to me. "What's wrong with him?"

"He's still a new ghost, so he hasn't formed all the way yet. Go ahead and talk to him. He won't hurt you."

Harold's chubby cheeks bounced as he hovered in the air before us. "All I wanted was to see you one last time," he confessed. "To tell you I love you, and I'm sorry I wasn't around."

Kelley let out a little laugh and swiped at her freely flowing tears. "You didn't know about me. Not until the end."

I turned and saw Drake watching the scene unfold in awe. He and Kelley could both clearly see Harold, but no longer could they see Virginia. All this ghost business was terribly confusing. I doubted if I'd ever learn the exact rules that governed how they interacted with the world of the living.

"I should have spent more time with you once I did know, but I was scared I'd disappoint you. I thought we'd have more time."

Kelley choked on another sob but was all smiles now. "Me, too. But maybe now that you're back, we can—?"

Harold's light dimmed, and she stopped short. "No. I can't stay. I will watch out for you, but it will be from the other side."

"Why won't you stay here with me?" If Kelley had possessed a ghostly light, I expect it would have faded then, too.

"Because my business is completed." Harold spoke matter-of-factly, but I could see how much it pained him to deny his daughter's wishes. He had changed so much since just last night. Not only was he speaking full sentences, but he was remembering. Emoting. "You now know how much I love you and wish things could have been different. I've seen you again, and I've given Gracie my warning."

"Um, speaking of that," I interjected, raising one index finger to draw everyone's attention. "Virginia's bound now. She can't hurt us. Thank you for the warning. It helped, I think."

Harold raised his disconnected hands and steepled them in front of his face. His brow furrowed as he drifted toward the ceiling and looked down on both Kelley and me. "No, my message was not about her, but another. One who still lives," he said at last, using the same strange voice as he had when first delivering this warning. "The seeds that were sown will soon bear dangerous fruits."

Kelley gasped, but little could surprise me at the moment.

"Yeah, can you give me more specific details? Like who, what, when, why? Any of that would help."

Harold dropped his hands and returned to

my eye level. His blue had become pale and much more transparent than before. "I've already said more than I should. The dead aren't supposed to interfere with the living. And also I don't remember enough to say."

He shifted his gaze back toward Kelley. "Stay well, my dear. I'll see you on the other side one day. Not too soon, though, okay?"

Kelley stretched her fingers out and touched her father's ghostly hand.

He bobbed for a moment before fading from view.

"That was so cool," Drake said from his spot on the couch.

Kelley stumbled over to join him. "I can't believe that was my dad."

"He seems like a pretty decent guy," Drake enthused. "I take back every bad thing I ever said about him."

While those two kept each other company, I snuck into my bedroom and motioned for the cats to join me. Once we were all inside, I gently closed the door behind us.

"What do we do now?" I whispered to them in a sudden burst of desperation. "They both know about magic. Does that mean I'm going to prison?"

Merlin chuckled in delight. "The thing about that is..."

"We found a loophole," Luna exclaimed with a rumbling purr.

I looked from one cat to the other. Both seemed pleased as punch. "What are you guys talking about? What loophole?"

"Well, technically Virginia is the one who revealed magic to them both. Not you," Merlin shared with pride.

"And I only spoke to Drake after she'd shown the true nature of her powers," Luna added. "Which means you won't be punished."

I was so relieved, I could almost feel the heavy emotional burden as it lifted from my shoulders.

"Neither of us will," Luna said with a Cheshire grin.

I let out a slow, long exhale. Ah, it felt so good. "Awesome. Well done. But what do we do now?"

"Gracie, we have a plan," Merlin promised, then motioned for me to lean closer so he could share all the details.

28

As it turned out, the cats really had thought of everything. While neither of them had ever possessed the magic to alter memories—that was an illusion witch specialty—Luna was able to successfully guide Merlin in brewing a powerful sleep potion.

They prepared it in gas form so it would be far easier to administer to our subjects. And once Drake and Kelley were out cold, Merlin teleported the lot of us back to Kelley's new house.

Virginia's old furniture hadn't been cleared out yet, so we moved both of our sleeping beauties to the floral-print couch. I took extra care to position them snuggled together with

Drake's head in Kelley's lap. Just in case that helped to get him thinking about her as a potential girlfriend.

Our primary hope, though, was that they'd wake up in the morning and believe everything that had occurred was nothing more than a crazy dream, one they'd somehow managed to create and move through concurrently.

I, of course, would deny any involvement in their ghostly adventures. While I hated gaslighting my friends, it really was for their protection—and sanity.

It would have been nice to have human friends with whom I could share my magical comings and goings, but it would be selfish of me to expose them to any long-term risks that came with knowing. Without any witches to claim and protect them, they would be on their own and, thus, in grave peril. At least that's what the cats told me.

Anyway, Kelley and Drake both had enough to keep them busy with how popular the newly improved Harold's House of Coffee had already proven to be.

The day after our great nocturnal adventures, Kelley was scheduled for another double shift with the new hires set to help during the morning rush and me and Drake to join her later in the morning. Yeah, she'd definitely have to expand the staff again soon, but I trusted her intuition when it came to knowing when to act.

And when I arrived to start work, I found Drake had already beaten me to it—something that had literally never happened before. I also found that he was holding hands with Kelley while she rang up a customer and one of the new staff members worked the espresso machine.

"Good morning!" I cried joyfully once they'd finished tending to the customer. "I got a great night's sleep and am ready for whatever today throws at us."

Okay, so maybe I was selling the ruse a little too hard, but they didn't know that. I'd taken great care with my eye makeup that morning to ensure not even the faintest of dark circles graced my visage. And now I would be chipper and upbeat for the entirety of my shift, no matter how much I wanted to crawl back into bed and sleep it off.

Drake yawned openly, refusing to let go of Kelley's hand. "What's so good about it?"

I nodded toward Kelley. "It seems like something's good. Or at least something's different."

They both blushed, and frankly, it was adorable.

Kelley motioned for me to come closer.

"We spent the night together last night. I don't remember him coming over, but when I woke up, there he was." She smiled as Drake pressed a kiss to her cheek. They'd really gone from zero to sixty in hardly any time at all.

"I don't remember, either," he said, "but that's not so unusual. I forget stuff I should know all the time and know stuff I shouldn't."

Kelley dropped her voice to a husky whisper. "The weirdest part, though, is that we both had the craziest dream. The same dream!"

"Really?" I squeaked, doing my best to imitate surprise.

"You were there, too," Drake pointed out as if he expected me to remember. "Did you by chance dream about ghosts and magic talking cats last night?"

I shook my head emphatically. "Nope. I slept like a log."

"Isn't it so funny how the little bits and pieces of daily life can fuse together to create this whole big adventure in the dream world?" Kelley asked, shaking her head. "Like my dad was there as a ghost! And there was this other ghost trying to hurt us, but Drake saved everyone. That's when my dad came and told me how much he loved me. I swear, you just mentioned ghosts one time as part of our icebreaking games, and it turns into this!"

"Yeah, and the wildest part is how we both dreamed the same thing," Drake said, narrowing his eyes at me. "The exact same thing."

"That is pretty wild." I nodded toward their joined hands. "It seems to have brought you together, though."

"Kelley's a pretty cool chick. Or should I say, pretty and cool," Drake responded before giving her little butterfly kisses with his eyelashes.

I was happy for them but also felt like if the pumpkin spice didn't make me puke today, their sickeningly sweet antics might.

"I've gotta go do the shift-end debrief with the new guys," Kelley announced with a sigh. "Be back soon."

Drake accepted a quick peck on the cheek and wiggled his fingers goodbye, watching her the whole way as she sauntered back toward the office.

"So you and Kelley?" I asked, not even trying to hide how happy I was about this turn of events.

"I know it wasn't a dream," Drake told me in a raspy whisper. "And I know you know it, too."

"I have no idea what you're talking about," I said with a shrug, then flipped my hair and went to wipe down the tables.

All the while I was panicking on the inside. How could he remember? And what would that mean for everyone going forward?

29

I returned home to two very happy cats and one very unhappy ghost. Merlin and Luna sat waiting for me on the kitchen table with huge matching grins spread between their whiskers while Virginia's nearly invisible form swooped around the house muttering muted curses.

"How's the new roommate settling in?" I asked the cats as Virginia swept toward me and then phased through me. Physically, I felt nothing, but it still felt like a violation.

I shuddered and yelled at her not to do that again.

"Or what?" the ghost asked so silently I had to strain to hear.

"Well, you are already grounded," I said with a laugh. "Give me time, though, I'll think of something."

Both cats laughed with me as Virginia disappeared into another part of the house.

"She hates it, and we love it," Merlin answered with bright eyes.

Luna seemed less amused despite her earlier laughter. "I still feel somewhat responsible for this all."

"You can't control the evil within someone else," I said, running my fingers over her smooth white fur. "And besides, now your children will know much more about ghosts than you ever did. That's a good thing, right?"

"I suppose," she said with a sigh and leaned into my touch.

"Never mind about that." Merlin stood and arched his back in a deep stretch. "We have a surprise for you."

I raised one eyebrow. "Oh?"

"Right this way, if you'll please."

Both cats hopped off the table and trotted down the hall to my bedroom. They stopped before entering, though.

"Look up," Merlin said with wide, eager eyes.

I looked up and saw nothing—or at least nothing that wasn't supposed to be there. And the sight of that plain, boring white ceiling made my heart leap with joy.

"You fixed it!" I cried, stooping down to pet both cats in thanks. "How? I thought you needed to go to Nocturna to find someone?"

"As much as I'd like to take credit, it was all Luna," Merlin announced with pride. "Tell her, Luna."

The she-cat looked embarrassed by her good deed. "Well, you know how we've been going to my garden so much lately?"

"I do."

"I figured if there were other garden witches nearby, they would have similarly well-stocked gardens." She paused, and Merlin picked up where his partner left off.

"We spent all day teleporting to various neighborhoods around the state until at last we found what we were looking for two towns over. A place called Beech Grove. There we met a magical human of all things! The garden was his, but he introduced us to a cat he knew named Mr. Fluffikins."

"And Mr. Fluffikins came with us and fixed the roof with just a swish of his tail. Can you believe it?" Luna cried. If I didn't know any better, I'd say this Fluffikins had left quite the impression on her.

Merlin didn't seem the least bit jealous, though, and I admired how secure their relationship had become after its rough start.

"I can't believe you went through all that for me. Thank you."

"Well, it was Merlin's fault, but now he knows better than to summon lightning indoors. Right, dear?" Luna glared at him.

Merlin's head drooped toward his chest. "Yes, dear."

"I appreciate you making it up to me, thank you." I gave them each another pat on the head before rising back to my feet.

"Oh, that's not him making it up to you," Luna said in a stern voice, directed more at Merlin than at me. "That's just setting things right. Merlin has another surprise for you as part of his apology, though."

Merlin took a deep breath. "I thought a lot about our talk the other day, and how important it is to you that Luna and I embrace human customs while living in the human world..." His words drifted off, leaving me confused. What was he getting at?

Luna nudged him with the side of her paw. "Well, go ahead. No need to dilly-dally."

The Maine Coon raised his head and regarded me with glowing green eyes. "And as such, Luna and I have decided to get married. Officially. Before the kittens come."

I clapped my hands together in excitement. "You guys, that's great! I'm so happy for—"

"And you will plan it for us," Luna gushed. "Isn't that wonderful?"

My smile faltered for a moment. "Uh, you guys don't have to do all this on my account." Especially if you expect me to do all the work, I added silently. I'd never planned a human wedding before, let alone a cat wedding. Where did one even begin?

"Think nothing of it, dear. We want to do this for you," Luna assured me. She really had no idea.

"Thanks," I said, trying so hard to keep some form of a smile plastered on my face. "When is the happy day?"

"This weekend!" they both cried in unison.

Oh, boy.

30

*A*nd so one adventure came to a close while many others loomed large on the horizon. I had a cat wedding to plan posthaste, a litter of kittens on the way in less than two months, a ghostly roommate I now needed to work hard at avoiding for the rest of my mortal existence, and the big bad was still out there.

I had no doubt we'd see Dash again, especially given Harold's eerie warning about sown seeds and dangerous fruit. Still, we had no idea how to find her, which meant we'd have to wait for her to come to us.

In the meanwhile, Merlin and I would just have to work to become as strong as possible so that we'd be ready when she returned. Thanks to Virginia's drain, I'd lost a good portion of the magic I'd accumulated since becoming Merlin's familiar. Luckily, my witchy cat was able to patch me up just fine. I had also started taking on magic faster the more and more time we spent together.

Everything would be fine. I had to believe that, or I would most assuredly go crazy.

The one thing that bothered me most about everything we'd just gone through, however, wasn't the near-death experience at the hands of an enemy I thought had been killed once and for all. It was the fact that my current coworker and former admirer Drake now knew about me and my cats—and who knows what else?

He had special abilities that none of us did, and he took them all in stride. The ghost hadn't weirded him out or broken his cool. He'd treated it like everything else in his life, somewhat interesting but mostly just... normal.

I longed to ask him what he was, but I figured he'd have no problem telling me if he actually knew himself.

He definitely knew what I was, though.

And he often tried to talk to me about that night's events when we found ourselves alone at work.

Let me tell you, the tabletops at Harold's had never looked shinier, thanks to all the good polishes I gave them whenever I needed an excuse to avoid him.

For now, Drake was taking care to speak to me only when we were guaranteed privacy, but what if he started blabbing to others? Would I be held responsible by magical law enforcement and forced to pay for this exposure?

Merlin and Luna had said I was in the clear since Virginia was the one who exposed herself to him, but I still felt sick about him knowing.

I trusted him with my safety, but my secrets?

Not a chance.

I had a feeling I'd need to make some very difficult choices soon in order to protect him, my magical family, and myself.

And with a sweet, innocent litter of nieces and nephews on the way, I couldn't afford to make any mistakes...

You already know that Gracie and Merlin's magical adventures are far from over. Ready to find out what happens next?

CLICK HERE to get your copy of Merlin Kills a Zombie so that you can keep reading this series today!

And make sure you're on Molly's list so that you hear about all the new releases, monthly giveaways, and other cool stuff (including lots and lots of cat pics).

**You can do that here:
MollyMysteries.com/subscribe**

WHAT'S NEXT?

When my cat brought me a dead bird as a present, I cringed.

When that dead bird suddenly flitted back to life, I screamed.

At first, I shrugged it off as one of the random things that happens when your roommate is a magical cat, but then it kept happening.

Turns out a familiar foe is creating an army of undead creatures with the goal of forcing us to surrender. But Merlin and I refuse to let dark magic prevail—not when the entire existence of magic is now at stake.

And if magic dies, so too will all who wield it.

Oh no, my cat will NOT become a casualty in this unholy war. I'm ready to fight my way through a million zombies and then take out the big bad, too. Nothing can come between this witchy cat and his familiar—and I'm ready to prove it.

MERLIN KILLS A ZOMBIE is now available.

CLICK HERE to get your copy so that you can keep reading this series today!

A BONUS SHORT

If you've never been to a magical cat wedding, then you are definitely missing out! But with so many supernatural creatures gathered in one small space, there's bound to be a kerfuffle or two. Luckily, Gracie Springs, resident human, wedding planner, and familiar extraordinaire, is on the case.

LUNA THE MAGICKLESS FLUFF is coming this fall as part of a special cozy mystery anthology. Subscribe to Molly's newsletter so you don't miss it!

You can do that here: MollyMysteries.com/subscribe

MEET MR. FLUFFIKINS

If you love Gracie and Merlin's magical antics, then you should meet Tawny and Mr. Fluffikins. Read on for a sneak peek of WITCH FOR HIRE, the first book in my Paranormal Temp Agency series...

My name is Tawny Bigford. I'm 35, single, and I love hot showers. Seriously, all I wanted was a hot shower to start my day off right, but when I went to confront my landlady about the broken plumbing, I wound up talking to her corpse instead.

Now everyone thinks I'm to blame for her murder—not the best way to make an impression on the new neighbors, let me tell you. But how can I prove I'm innocent when I know practically nothing about the woman I supposedly killed?

Especially not the fact that she was the official Beech Grove Town Witch. Her former boss—a snarky black cat named Mr. Fluffikins—says I have to fill her vacated role until the real killer can be caught and brought to justice.

So, whether I like it or not, I've just been recruited to the Paranormal Temp Agency. Now I need to solve my landlady's murder, figure out how to wield my newly granted powers, and maybe even find a way to fit in around here.

Yup. All in a day's work for this novice witch.

WITH FOR HIRE is now available.

CLICK HERE to get your copy so that you can start reading this series today. You can also turn the page to read the first chapter...
Enjoy!

"Aaaaaaaaaah!" A scream tore from my chest as I leaped away from the frigid stream gushing out of the old showerhead.

Normally I loved starting my mornings with a slow and steamy rinse while I let all of my thoughts boing around my brain and eventually meld themselves into some kind of plan for the day. Ever since moving to Beech Grove a couple weeks back, however, I was lucky to get a good five minutes of warmth before the water heater suddenly gave up the ghost and a punishing spray of liquid ice ruined my good mood.

"That's it!" I shouted as I twisted the faucet off. My landlady would be hearing from me today, whether she liked it or not.

For her part, old Mrs. Haberdash had given me very careful instructions when I signed up to rent the small guest home at the back edge of her hilltop property. Even though she lived in the main house, just a short walk away, I was never ever supposed to visit her there. Anything I needed could be explained via a phone call or better yet—*at least according to her*—an old-fashioned letter.

Yeah, no.

I tried to do it her way, but so far my attempts at getting help with the plumbing had gone unanswered, and unfortunately, a useless shower made for a useless me. I'd tried playing by her rules and still had nothing to show for it. Now it was a time to play by mine.

Still dripping, I bunched my soapy hair into a bun to get it off my shoulders, threw on a shift dress and flip-flops, and headed out to finally confront my apathetic landlady.

I guess now would be a good time to introduce myself.

The name's Tawny, Tawny Bigford. Tawny is short for *Tanya,* a name I've hated ever since Tanya Mills stuck a chewed-up wad of bubble gum in my hair during our second grade spelling test. So now I'm Tawny.

I'm 35, love my showers—as you already know—and am wonderfully, happily, unapologetically single.

Sure, I had a husband once. George was his name. But several years into our marriage, he decided he made a much better pair with some PTA mom named Patricia.

A PTA mom!

As the story goes, they'd bumped into each other outside of the local middle school one afternoon, and it was love at first sight. Why George was there in the first place, I'll never understand. It's not like we had kids of our own or any other reason for him to find himself at exactly the wrong place and wrong time.

But it happened and changed all of our lives in the process.

Honestly, I'd have rather he slipped off with his younger, prettier secretary. At least then I could bemoan the cliche.

But he and Patricia, who is two years his senior, are disgustingly happy together. Most days I just pretend that neither of them exists.

Okay, so I may sound *a little* bitter. And I may live by myself in a rented guest house, but —disappointing showers not withstanding—I absolutely love my life. Basically I write two books per year, ship them off to my publisher for a paycheck, and then do whatever I want with the rest of my time.

Yes, I could write more to make more, but

why? I'm perfectly happy to live frugally because that means living freely. And as such, I have more hobbies than any one person should probably ever have.

But I digress...

This wasn't the time to discuss my hobbies, it was the time to confront Mrs. Haberdash and to demand a steady supply of hot water that lasted more than five minutes per day. It was, after all, a simple and basic necessity.

On her doorstep now, I sucked in a deep breath to calm my rage, raised my hand, and knocked gently.

Just kidding, I pounded on that door with every bit of ire I had in me.

When no one answered, I started to shout. "I know you're in there! And I need to talk!"

Still nothing, so I tried the doorknob and was surprised to find it unlocked, given how much I knew the woman valued her privacy.

I pushed it open and charged in, ready to give old Mrs. Haberdash a piece of my mind.

Unfortunately, while all this righteous storming was going on, I hadn't kept an eye on my feet. I hadn't thought I needed to, but something big and heavy was lying on the ground just beyond the threshold and I slammed right into it, lost my balance, and thudded to the ground in an awkward tangle of limbs.

Not just my own, but Mrs. Haberdash's, too. *Uh-oh.* My stomach churned with an aching certainty.

"M-M-Mrs. Haberdash?" I asked, my voice quavering with fright as I turned my face toward the old woman sprawled across the entryway floor.

Her mouth remained firmly closed, her eyes glued open, her body even colder than the shower I'd just escaped.

Yup, she was dead, and—thanks to my unfortunate stumble—I'd just gotten my DNA all over her corpse.

No, no, no! I attempted a scream but came up short.

And here I thought a cold shower was the absolute worst way to start the day. Oh, when would I ever learn to leave well enough alone?

WITH FOR HIRE is now available.

CLICK HERE to get your copy so that you can start reading this series today!

MORE MOLLY

ABOUT MOLLY FITZ

While USA Today bestselling author Molly Fitz can't technically talk to animals, she and her doggie best friend, Sky Princess, have deep and very animated conversations as they navigate their days. Add to that, five more dogs, a snarky feline, comedian husband, and diva daughter, and you can pretty much imagine how life looks at the Casa de Fitz.

Molly lives in a house on a high hill in the Michigan woods and occasionally ventures out for good food, great coffee, or to meet new animal friends.

Writing her quirky, cozy animal mysteries

is pretty much a dream come true, but sometimes she also goes by the names Melissa Storm and Mila Riggs and writes a very different kind of story.

Learn more, grab the free app, or sign up for her newsletter at **www.MollyMysteries.com**!

PET WHISPERER P.I.

Angie Russo just partnered up with Blueberry Bay's first ever talking cat detective. Along with his ragtag gang of human and animal helpers, Octo-Cat is determined to save the day... so long as it doesn't interfere with his schedule. Start with book 1, ***Kitty Confidential***.

PARANORMAL TEMP AGENCY

Tawny Bigford's simple life takes a turn for the magical when she stumbles upon her landlady's murder and is recruited by a talking black cat named Fluffikins to take over the deceased's role as the official Town Witch for Beech Grove, Georgia. Start with book 1, **Witch for Hire**.

MERLIN THE MAGICAL FLUFF

Gracie Springs is not a witch... but her cat is. Now she must help to keep his secret or risk spending the rest of her life in some magical prison. Too bad trouble seems to find them at every turn! Start with book 1, **Merlin the Magical Fluff.**

THE MEOWING MEDIUM

Mags McAllister lives a simple life making candles for tourists in historic Larkhaven, Georgia. But when a cat with mismatched eyes enters her life, she finds herself with the ability to see into the realm of spirits... Now the ghosts of people long dead have started coming to her for help solving their cold cases. Start with book 1, **Secrets of the Specter.**

THE PAINT-SLINGING SLEUTH

Following a freak electrical storm, Lisa Lewis's vibrant paintings of fairytale creatures have started coming to life. Unfortunately, only she can see and communicate with them. And when her mentor turns up dead, this aspiring artist must turn amateur sleuth to clear her name and save the day with only these "pigments" of her imagination to help her. Start with book 1, **My Colorful Conundrum**.

SPECIAL COLLECTIONS

Black Cat Crossing
Pet Whisperer P.I. Books 1-3
Pet Whisperer P.I. Books 4-6
Pet Whisperer P.I. Books 7-9
Pet Whisperer P.I. Books 10-12

CONNECT WITH MOLLY

You can download my free app here:
mollymysteries.com/app

Or sign up for my newsletter and get a special digital prize pack for joining, including an exclusive story, Meowy Christmas Mayhem, fun quiz, and lots of cat pictures!
mollymysteries.com/subscribe

Have you ever wanted to talk to animals? You can chat with Octo-Cat and help him solve an exclusive online mystery here:

mollymysteries.com/chat

Or maybe you'd like to chat with other animal-loving readers as well as to learn about new books and giveaways as soon as they happen! Come join Molly's VIP reader group on Facebook.

mollymysteries.com/group

MORE BOOKS LIKE THIS

Welcome to Whiskered Mysteries, where each and every one of our charming cozies comes with a furry sidekick... or several! Around here, you'll find we're all about crafting the ultimate reading experience. Whether that means laugh-out-loud antics, jaw-dropping magical exploits, or whimsical journeys through small seaside towns, you decide.

So go on and settle into your favorite comfy chair and grab one of our *paw*some cozy mysteries to kick off your next great reading adventure!

Visit our website to browse our books and meet our authors, to jump into our discussion group, or to join our newsletter. See you there!

www.WhiskeredMysteries.com

WHISKMYS (WĬSK′MƏS)

DEFINITION : a state of fiction-induced euphoria that commonly occurs in those who read books published by the small press, Whiskered Mysteries.

USAGE: Every day is Whiskmys when you have great books to read!

**LEARN MORE AT
WWW.WHISKMYS.COM**